FORGING GLORY

FORGING
BOOK 1

LAINEY DAVIS

By Lainey Davis

Join my newsletter and never miss a new release!

laineydavis.com

❀ Created with Vellum

For Jenni Hermoso
#ContigoJenni

CONTENT NOTE

This book contains inappropriate and harassing behavior from a male character in a position of power. Some readers may find his actions and the dynamics disturbing or uncomfortable. Please read with discretion.

The author in no way condones this type of conduct. The character's behavior represents an unfortunate reality for many women and people of marginalized genders. His characterization aims to bring awareness to systemic issues in sports culture and society as a whole.

While the depicted events are fictional, their impact is very real. If you find this content too upsetting, you may want to pass on this title. Please take care of yourself.

ABOUT THIS BOOK

My only dream was going pro ... until she blazed back into my life.

Cara Moreno - my biggest regret - just signed with the women's soccer team in my city. I tell myself to keep my distance ... but I can't stay away.

She says the most powerful man in the sport is set on destroying her career. That behind closed doors, he's hurting her and everything she's worked for.

I doubted her once before and rejected her. Now, I'll do anything to make things right and protect what's ours.

Exposing the truth means risking my career. But how can I chase my dreams knowing hers are slipping away?

With both our futures on the line, I'm ready to risk it all and expose the truth. Losing her once was devastating enough. I won't let her down a second time.

What we share is electric and protecting her feels worth any sacrifice. This time, I'll fight for her trust...and hopefully her heart.

A high-stakes, sizzling sports romance, Forging Glory delivers courage, second chances, and a fight for love against all odds.

CHAPTER 1
WES

I'M ALONE.

I'm aware of that reality before I'm fully awake in a room where I should have the gorgeous body of Cara Moreno draped over my chest.

I can't fight the disappointment that simmers, even though I know what last night was to both of us. It was a celebration. Releasing a pressure valve. We both have a lot riding on the camp from this weekend and riding each other was a celebration and a release.

Except, it didn't feel that way to me.

I did things with Cara that I've never done before, never wanted to do. I felt like we had a connection and a lump forms in my throat realizing that was clearly a one-sided assumption. She didn't even leave a note. I reach for my phone to see if maybe she texted me, and it starts ringing in my hand.

Unknown number.

I have to answer it, in case it's an offer, but I'm not prepared for the volume that comes bellowing at me at ... I glance at the alarm clock ... 6:30.

"Wes! Baby!"

"Hello?"

"Don't you know my voice, kid? That's okay. Listen, your Uncle Hawk told me to give you a ring, said you're going to need me today."

I comb my memories, trying to place the too-chipper voice on the other end of the phone. "Brian?"

"The one and only." My uncle's sports agent starts praising my game, comparing me to the family legacy, whatever that means. I wake up more fully and start to process the meaning of his call.

"Wait. My uncle called you?"

"Damn right he did, and not a minute too soon. The sharks are swimming outside your door, baby."

I glance toward the hotel door and see a bunch of slips of paper on the carpet. Huh.

"Listen," Brian continues. "I'm not going to dance around. You know I was a good partner for your Uncle Hawky and made him a shit-ton of money over the years. I can guarantee you the same treatment and the second you sign an agreement I can text you. I can be on the phone with those sharks in the lobby of your hotel. Where do you want to land, Wesley? Name your team."

I drag a hand through my hair. "Name my team? Seriously?"

He sighs. "Okay, not quite that awesome. But give me a ranked list. Word on the street is your debut will be electric."

If my uncle called his agent, that means Aunt Lucy wasn't kidding when she hinted that my "subterfuge" worked in my favor. I snuck out here to California against the advice of my parents and without their support. I gave up my college scholarship for this try-out and I almost can't believe the gamble paid off. My stomach flutters and I stand up, pacing the floor. I catch a glimpse of myself in the mirror, with obvious sex-tousled hair, swollen lips, and scratch marks on my chest.

Cara sticking around to celebrate would have been too good to be true.

Last night she made me feel like I can do anything, achieve anything I want.

This morning, it's all happening … but she's not here. And neither is my family.

I sigh as Brian talks about numbers and sponsorship plans. It all sounds great, actually. So maybe it was better to have one perfect night than keep things going and grow frustrated with one another. We both will be diving headfirst into intense schedules and camera shoots and too much travel. That's no way to kick off a relationship.

"Sounds perfect, Brian. Text me the thing to sign."

I feel a pang of sadness that my dad isn't here with me when I sign my first contract with an agent, that I'll most likely be signing with a pro team in a few hours without my family celebrating. My Aunt Alice would have made a grain-free cake out of vegetables or some shit. My cousins would have gotten kazoos and done a damn parade around the Highland Park fountain if I'd looped them in.

Or they wouldn't have done anything. My mom would have cried and my dad would have glowered at me, and I would have stayed in school another year. If I'd stayed in school, who even knows what would have happened. I probably would have blown my ACL. I can't grieve what didn't happen any more than I can regret my choices.

Brian texts me an agreement and I sign it with my finger on my cell phone, alone in a dark hotel room.

A few seconds later, Brian texts me instructions to head down to the lobby in twenty minutes, and he'll video chat in while I have a conference with an offer. And there it is: my new life … the one I worked hard for. The one I set in motion.

I should want to call my cousins, or the guys from my college team, but the first person I think of is Cara. Did she get a similar offer this morning? Should I find her room and go another round with her to celebrate, possibly real quick before we both fly out? Does she have an agent? Maybe I should send her Brian's contact info…

These thoughts swirl in my mind as I brush my teeth and slip into the only clean clothes I have left, sweats and an old Pittsburgh Forge t-shirt of my Uncle's.

I step out of the elevator on the ground floor and turn the corner, toward the conference rooms. I'm about to video call Brian when I see something that halts me in my tracks.

Lou Rubeo, president of Soccer USA, has a hand on Cara's shoulder, his lips a centimeter from her ear. I watch as his other hand moves to brush a hair back from her face, the same face I had my lips all over just hours before.

I feel nauseated, watching this man put his hands on the woman of my dreams. I guess if she can sneak out of my bed and into his arms an hour later, she's not the woman I thought she was.

I don't know why she is going for a high-powered soccer executive, and I don't have time to care. She's on her path and I'm on mine. I'm glad she's not looking toward me. I am glad she doesn't see my face as I stab the call button for my agent.

I turn on my heel and walk toward the conference room.

CHAPTER 2
CARA
ONE MONTH LATER

MY ROOMMATE, Jay, slides down the hall of our apartment in her socks, singing some wake-up song she says she learned at camp as a kid. I throw a pillow at her from my bed. "I'm going to start sleeping with the door closed if you keep doing that."

She pokes her head into my room, a toothbrush dangling from her mouth. "You should probably sleep with the door closed anyway, Moreno. What's wrong with you?"

"Remember how I said my parents were deep into Catholic school dogma?" I shrug, sitting up in bed. "I wasn't ever allowed to close my bedroom door except when I was changing. I guess it's hard to break that habit."

In college I had three roommates from my soccer team. We called ourselves the Midfield Mamis, and we lived in a two-bedroom apartment near campus. I'm not sure if we closed our bedroom doors then because we all went to bed super early or if we passed out exhausted from training and study ing. Jay continues brushing feverishly as I try to gather my hair off my face. I swear it got bigger as I slept or else it's just making itself at home in the Pittsburgh humidity. I'm told I'll get used to the weather here—balmy one minute, windy the next, but rarely sunny.

Jay rolls her eyes. "We can make our own house rules now, Cara. Ones that make sense!" She slides away, humming as she finishes her dental scrub. She and I are rookies on the Pittsburgh Hot Metal. We met at the tryout camp a month ago and I was excited when she asked if I wanted to find a place with her near the stadium in Pittsburgh.

I kick my door closed and change into workout gear. I can't stop smiling as I pull on the black socks, shorts, and t-shirt for my team. I want to pinch myself and make sure this is real, that I am actually a professional soccer player.

This has been my goal, my dream, for as long as I can remember. And now that it's here, I love that I still have goals, things to work toward. I want to start in a game and score for my team. I want to be chosen for the national team and play in the Olympics.

Everything I've ever wanted relates to soccer, to physical achievement and competition. I remind myself of this each time I think of that try-out weekend in California. When I secured my spot on this team. That weekend I also met someone I could very well have lost myself to.

It would have been easy to fall into Wesley Stag. I could bask under his intense gaze, writhe in pleasure as he strummed my body for hours. Everything was intensified with Wes, and the way he focused on my pleasure…it shook something inside me.

Growing up under such strict rules meant sex—even solo sex—was forbidden and had to be a stolen moment. It took me years to own my sexuality and that night with Wes was an epic, shattering explosion of pleasure.

I snort and slam my dresser drawer shut because those hours were short-lived. He made that very clear by refusing to answer my calls or respond to any of my texts.

Ghosted.

Ditched like the one-and-done I should have assumed I was to him. I brush my teeth and weave my curls into a long braid, definitely not thinking about the slide of Wes's fingers running through my hair, massaging my scalp.

"You ready to head out?" Jay jangles her car keys in the hall, pulling me from my heated reminiscing.

"Yep. Wait. I need protein."

I pull my door open and grin when I see my roommate holding one of the egg muffins we prepped on our day off. We filled cupcake tins with scrambled eggs, turkey sausage, feta cheese, and spinach, so we'd have a quick breakfast that met all our nutrition guidelines from Coach Lucy.

The fact that we both eat them cold while leaving the apartment at the last possible second solidifies our status as best roommates ever. Some women wake up early to perfect their makeup. Jay and I sleep in and bond over food. We operate in practiced efficiency as we approach the car, me holding both our bags and tossing them in the back seat while Jay navigates her keys, muffin, and coffee mug, still humming camp songs.

The September sun is just starting to rise as Jay's Honda pulls into the lot outside the stadium. The women's team has the field first today, and I love our cardio session by the river. We run laps and agility ladders as the freight trains roll past. We sprint in intervals as the tugboats blast their horns behind the coal barges chugging up the Monongahela River.

I feel part of the industry here, maybe because my team is named for the liquid iron still manufactured in the valleys nearby. When Coach tells us to start running the steps in the stadium, my legs threaten to liquefy from the exertion. But I remind myself that I am forged of strong will. I fought to get here. I'll fight to stay here.

The whistle blows, signifying the end of morning work-out, and I sink into one of the benches near the grass. One of the trainers tosses me a drink, and I shield my eyes from the sun as I chug it down, watching as the men's team takes the field.

And of course I see him. My regrettable dalliance, Wesley Stag, plays striker for the men's team here. I can't let go of what happened in part because I see him every damn day at work, and the hot dummy doesn't even look at me.

I suck down the rest of my drink, glaring at him, until Lucy waves us all to join her in the tunnel. "I'm turning you over to Coach Ben, folks. I believe you have film next, then lunch and afternoon drills." She pats her clipboard and waves as we all pull off our sneakers.

———

I must carry a sour look on my face the rest of the day, because Jay asks me about it on the way home. "You're usually in a better mood after chicken teriyaki." She lowers the volume on the radio, inviting me to spill my guts as we navigate traffic on the Fort Pitt Bridge.

I can't help the sigh that rumbles out of me as I plunk my head against my window. "I saw Wes again today. He didn't look at me."

"That guy again? Come on, Cara. He's not worth all this space in your head."

"I know that, but it's easy to *say* I'll forget about him after he ghosted me, and it's another thing to literally see him every day and experience him not even making eye contact. I actually think I might be invisible to him."

"You're the furthest thing from invisible."

"Thanks, friend. If it helps, I do hate that I'm fixated like this."

Jay taps the steering wheel and chews on her lip for a few blocks. "Have you considered that, this…" She gestures toward my face. "Might be more about something else than it is about what's-his-name?"

"You know his name is Wesley."

"Only because you don't shut the hell up about him. But seriously, what about talking to Big Jim?"

I groan a little at her reference to our sports psychologist. He leads multiple sessions a week about mindset and trusting our teammates, and the content is always inspiring. It's just that Jim blinks. A lot.

"Do you think I could I talk to him over the phone?"

She shrugs. "It's not a bad idea. I mean, he's there. He's a resource. Maybe email him?"

I pop my lips a few times, considering. I haven't cemented a starting spot in the lineup yet. Maybe this hang-up on Wes is holding me back somehow. I clench my stomach, trying to ignore the voice in my gut wondering if Jay is on to something about my issues running deeper than Wes ignoring me.

Because I probably do know why he ghosted me, and I don't want to remember the slimy sensation freezing me in space as Lou Rubeo, the president of Soccer USA, invaded my personal space at the hotel and served me a huge helping of the creeps when he touched me. The last time I made eye contact with Wesley Stag was the moment Rubeo ran an uninvited finger down my face.

"I'm going to talk it out with my chicas. They'll probably tell me to call Big Jim, too."

"When are those chicas going to find me a lady-friend? There are not enough lesbians in Pittsburgh."

"Toni hooked you up with a cheering section when we traveled to Chicago last week."

Jay grins and waggles her eyebrows. "Exactly. Remind me where the rest of them live?"

Jay parks in the garage under our building and I rattle off the current locations of my friend group, texting them as I walk to let them know I need one of our chats.

By the time Shante replies from D.C., she's already spoken to Rose and Toni.

SHANTE

Emergency video pedis, 10am east coast tomorrow.

TONI

That's 7 for you, Rosie-bug

ROSALIE

Excuse me, I am a very important PhD candidate studying insects. I am not personally an insect.

"Jay, we're doing pedicures tomorrow. You in?"

"Hell no, I'm not in." She shouts from her room and then I hear the shower turn on.

I holler louder and I know she hears me tease, "Fine. Keep your rhino hide, but don't ask me how to meet more single ladies."

She pokes a head into the hall, clutching a towel around her tattooed chest. "You really think it's my feet?"

I laugh and shake my head. "I mean, nobody wants that rough sandpaper with them in bed."

"Ugh. Fine. I will exfoliate but I'm not doing polish." She slams the door as I confirm that I'm in for video pedicures.

We Midfield Mamis have been doing this for years—sitting for hours and massaging our feet while we unload everything weighing on our minds. We slough off bad vibes along with dry skin and finish the whole procedure with pampered toes and unburdened souls.

My college friends have retired from soccer, moved on to graduate school and corporate America. But they're still my safe place. I should open up to them about what's been going on, and I don't quite understand why I haven't.

I don't want to douse Jay with cold water by running a competing shower, so I wait for her to finish her scrub. We could shower at the stadium, but both of us prefer the luxury of our own bathrooms. It's the best part of this apartment, apart from the proximity to the water we can see from our balcony.

Each bedroom has an ensuite bathroom. It feels decadent.

I step onto my little piece of paradise, aka the balcony, while I wait for my turn with the hot water heater.

It's not much. All I have out here is a folding chair and a few plants that should be hung, but I haven't had a chance to buy stands or install hooks. And it's mine.

I'm here despite my parents' disapproval. I'm here regardless of their insistence that I'll never meet "a nice boy" to settle down and raise a family; that I am not putting my degree to use; that this career can't possibly bring lasting stability.

Those are their concerns, and their battles. I remind myself of this even as I hyper focus on the "nice boy" who did just as my parents said he would: turn his back on me.

CHAPTER 3
WES

"YOGA FOR ATHLETES" is not how I predicted I'd spend my afternoon while my professional soccer team travels to Louisville for a match without me, but Coach…my uncle… suggested I work on my flexibility to really give myself a chance at a roster spot.

It's been a bit of a blow to my pride coming into the team as a permanent bench warmer. When I left my senior year of college to sign with a professional team, I definitely thought I'd roll into town a star player. Until I prove myself, I spend my days as "generic defender" during drills while the starters work on game strategy. These days, it feels like everyone views me as generically expendable, from my coach on down to the woman I met at the tryout camp.

My career has to be my focus right now. There's only so much time to claw my way onto a professional soccer lineup and I'll do anything necessary to be one of those starters.

So here I am, running late as I make my way to Pipe Fitters, a fitness studio in the east end of the city where I'm told the staff is discreet and the clientele won't post pictures of me on social media.

Class is in session when I hustle in the door, and I kick off my shoes near the studio as I grab the last mat from the bin. I try to shake it open somewhere in the back row, but the teacher smiles and waves me toward a spot near the front.

My knees lock when I see that, of course, the space is next to Cara Moreno. Great.

It's been bad enough trying to avoid her at the stadium for the past month while everyone raves about how great she is on the field. Now I have to pretend she didn't stomp all over my emotions as we sit side by side and open our chakras, or whatever we're doing in yoga class.

I could leave now, watch a yoga video on YouTube or something, but I want to play professional soccer more than I want to avoid this woman, so I grunt, adjust my shorts, and plop the mat into place as the teacher welcomes us all to take our place.

Cara doesn't see me yet because she's bent over, stretching with her perfect ass in the air. My brain immediately flashes to an image of me behind her in the shower, Cara bent over just like that as I soaped her spine and played with her clit.

Cara finally looks at me as I settle in. I try to keep my face neutral and look forward, but I see her in my periphery. She appears … hurt. Confused? Screw that.

"This will be a restorative practice, meant to open your hips, relax your spine, and ease those knots in your busy shoulders." The teacher's voice is soothing as she paces the floor between the rows of mats. It occurs to me that maybe yoga is the secret sauce that keeps Cara in her starting spot, even as a rookie.

A quick glance around shows me a few pro football guys, a hockey player I recognize. I feel better, more at ease knowing I'm among likeminded professional athletes. Do I even get to call myself that since I haven't played one minute of pro soccer yet? If my uncle thinks this will get me where I need to be, I'll fold my foot in half and drag a knuckle down my arch like the teacher suggests.

As I work my toes apart, I keep seeing Cara from the corner of my eye. Her toes are painted burgundy now, and I wish I wasn't thinking about how beautifully that color contrasts with her tan skin.

"Give each of your toes a little tug and feel the blood moving into them." The teacher pats me on the shoulder gently, pulling my concentration back to the intense stretch in my feet. The last time I played with a foot, it was Cara's. And now I'm hard in yoga class thinking about her toes in my mouth.

I'm relieved when we switch to some hip opener poses, even more so when we rotate so I'm facing away from her. Until I realize this means she's staring at my ass as I widen my stance and hinge my hips forward.

It's fair to say my concentration is not where it needs to be if I'm going to draw the full benefit from this class, and I try my best to focus on my breath, to listen to the instructor. Until she says we are going to rely on a partner for the next series of hip poses.

I close my eyes, willing her to pair me with the linebacker on my right instead of the gorgeous woman messing with my feelings. "Cara, I'm going to ask you to team up with our newcomer today, if that's alright with you?"

I feel the teacher's hand on my arm as she turns me toward my one night stand. Cara pinches her lips together, looking everywhere but into my eyes. Whatever. I lie on my back with my knees bent and my feet on the floor, staring at the ceiling like I'm about to endure a medical procedure. When instructed, I pull one knee toward my chest and tip my foot toward the ceiling, wondering where the partner part comes into play.

"Okay, class. Let's have our standing yogi press a palm into our stretching partner's foot. Yes, just like that, Dustin. See how Jameel's hip is slowly stretching?"

I refuse to look as Cara's palm connects with the arch of

my foot. I close my eyes, accepting this delicious stretch, but I can't focus on it too much because my junk is going to create a problem. By the time we switch to the other side, I'm fully erect and I open my eyes to see Cara kneeling between my legs. Her face hovers a foot above my crotch as she presses onto my foot.

My eyes connect with hers and I know she knows how my body is responding. If I had any say in the matter, I'd be flaccid, or better yet, I wouldn't be here at all.

A cramp burns in my lower back and I groan, rolling out of the stretch and rocking back and forth on the mat until the teacher arrives to talk me through a pose that releases the pain. Mercifully, she sticks by me for the remainder of the poses.

But at some point, I realize this leaves Cara to work with another partner, and I don't like it any better when I see a lanky dude pressing on *her* foot with his face hovering above her crotch. Why am I so messed up in the head over this woman? A bigger man would confront her, clear the air.

I'm not feeling very big as we pack up our mats, and I try to sneak out the way I came in, but I hear Cara's voice as I'm spritzing my mat with cleaner. "Can we talk?"

"I have nothing to say to you." I roll up the mat and start walking toward the bin near the exit.

"Five minutes, Wes, is all I'm asking. Then you can go back to ignoring me."

"Me, ignoring you?" I toss the mat into the bin with a muted thump. "That's rich, considering your attention span when it comes to men."

She shakes her head. "I knew you thought that. I knew you had misinterpreted what you saw. That's why you ghosted me when I could have really used a friend."

"Oh, you found a friend all right."

Once more, my memory is active, pulling up the cozy scene I walked in on as I went to sign my contract with the

Forge. I saw his hand on her cheek as she stood there with no bra, probably still smelling like sex. With me.

Cara's face contorts as if I've slapped her. She clutches at her stomach and grips the wall with one hand. She swallows and shakes her head. "I can't believe I thought we could talk this out."

She pushes past me toward the exit. "Go on and leave then, Moreno. Again." I know I'm being a dick, but I can't seem to control myself.

Cara stops and looks over her shoulder at me, and I'm a little surprised to see her eyes welling with tears. She wipes her face and shoves the studio door open, leaving me alone in the hall.

Her tears give me pause. They seem out of character from what I know about her. Cara entered that tryout camp feisty and confident. She knew exactly what she wanted that entire weekend and made no bones about grabbing everything from multiple scouts' attention to my junk in a vice grip. And she left with a pro soccer contract, so something worked in her favor.

I don't know what to make of her outburst, but I don't have time to dwell on it anyway. My own career is on the brink of collapse. She did me a favor when she made sure our one night stayed that way.

CHAPTER 4
CARA

I SLAM the apartment door so hard that Jay springs up from the couch where she'd evidently been napping. "Cara?" Her face wrinkles and I close my eyes, taking a deep breath.

"Yes. Sorry. I just got a little carried away."

She frowns and rubs the back of her neck, then clicks off the television. "I thought yoga was supposed to be relaxing."

I sink into the couch next to her. We have a rare day off today and were each assigned different active rest. "I wish I'd gotten your stretchy band workout instead."

Jay snorts. "Yeah, right. Because it's so relaxing to squat a thousand times while Coach Lucy controls the resistance."

"I'm guessing you didn't have to defend your honor to a pigheaded striker at least."

Jay sighs audibly. "Is this about your reindeer?"

I swat her with the pillow. "His name is Stag, weirdo."

She shrugs. "It's funnier to call him a reindeer. Especially if he's being a douche."

I open my mouth to protest but my phone chirps with an incoming text. I glance at the screen and see that it's from Toni, whom I forgot I was supposed to call this morning.

"And now he made me stand up my friends. I can't with this guy."

"Let it out, Moreno. Get it over with."

I elbow her again and prop the phone up on the coffee table, clicking the icon to join the video chat in progress. All my chicas glare at me, pumice stones in hand and I wince.

"I forgot fancy-foot time. I'm so sorry."

Rosalie wags a finger at me. "I'm up at the crack of dawn! I don't do this for just anybody."

I grimace but Jay kicks my foot with her own. "We've got some rhino hide happening over here, folks."

Shante wags a finger at me. "That's what you get for leaving us in the lurch, chica. Did you even pre-soak and remove your polish from last time?"

I pry myself from the couch and scoot to my bathroom to grab my pedicure kit. When I get back to the living room, I'm touched to see that Jay got me a tub of warm water and a towel from the kitchen. "Go on," she whispers. "Shave your calluses like a block of parmesan cheese."

"You are disgusting, and I love it." Toni snickers from the tiny screen in the living room and I dunk my feet into the water. "One of these days we're gonna get you to join us," she shouts to Jay, who grunts and heads down the hall to her room.

She halts mid-stride and turns, poking her head back into the living room to shout, "Make sure she tells you about the reindeer. We have to get her to clear her head about that guy, no matter how great his antlers are."

I throw a pillow down the hall at her as she disappears into her room with another cackle.

When I look back at the screen, Rosalie is gesturing with her pumice stone. "Cara, babe, I can either tell you how my feet are starting to become real human feet now that I'm not running 30 miles a week in cleats, or I can remind you that you are working very hard to get selected for the national team leading up to the Olympics."

"Feet, please," I groan while my friends drown my voice in a chorus of "mm hmm."

"The fucking Olympics, Cara." Shante starts dabbing a cotton ball on her toes, scrubbing off last week's plum polish with gusto.

"Look." I cross an ankle over my lap and get to work with the callous shaver, noticing that my friends no longer even need to use this tool since, as they say, they've stopped playing soccer. They also don't get to spend their mornings watching the sun rise over the river. They no longer have world-class coaches helping them condition their bodies for maximum performance. But they know damn well how much these experiences mean to me.

"It's not like I was looking for him to be my boyfriend. I just really thought we connected and, well, it hurt my feelings when he ghosted me."

I bite my lip, feeling guilty that I'm not opening up to them about the added anguish of not knowing what to do about the creepy situation I found myself in with the president of Soccer USA. I don't even know how to explain it out loud, but I do know Wes Stag noticed something amiss. And instead of asking me my side of things, he jumped to the worst conclusion.

I get to work on my heels as I tell them about seeing Wes at yoga class. I leave out the details of how fine he looked in workout tights and a fitted t-shirt. "He's just … so done with me. And yet I have to see him every day."

Rosalie pulls a sympathetic face and leans close to her camera. "Cara, that sucks. What are the chances that your fresco hookup from camp would end up signed to the same city as you?"

Shante perks up. "Oh, I could tabulate the chances. How many pro women's teams are we up to now?"

"Thank you, stat doctor," Toni interrupts. "We don't need the actual numbers. What Rosalie is trying to say is that we know it stings to see him every day and think about that rejection. But we also know you will feel terrific once you do get past it. Like, are you seriously going to even think about him when Coach Akemi is handing you a red, white, and blue jersey?"

Rosalie nods. "Así es, chica."

Toni shakes a bottle of pink nail polish, rattling the little beads inside as she blends the colors. I reach for my matching shade as she asks, "You know what's better than a boyfriend, querida?"

Jay chooses that moment to re-enter the conversation, plunking next to me on the couch and shouting, "Literally everything." We all crack up laughing and I make room for her in front of the screen. Jay won't paint her nails, but she does reach for the lotion and starts to work on her feet.

"Seriously, though," Toni adds. "An Olympic gold medal will last a hell of a lot longer, look better around your neck, and open more doors for you than any boyfriend ever has."

As my friends erupt in a chorus of support and applause, I feel a lot better about the whole thing. After I end the video chat, Jay gives me a pointed look. "Do they still not know about how Lou Rubeo treated you?"

Her words feel like a slap. I shake my head and my mouth works up and down. "I haven't been able to find the words."

She frowns and places a hand on my shoulder. "The way he was getting in your space in the hall at lunch in California? That wasn't okay, Cara. I saw how he was looking at you, and that's not how professionals assess one another."

I blink rapidly in disbelief. I remember that Jay had come around the corner the very first time I encountered the soccer president. His actions that day had made me uncomfortable. Jay doesn't even mention how he escalated his creep factor, and the fact that she remembers even the one indiscretion makes me shaky.

My eyes start watering, and my chest feels tight. "Jay, he's …" I think about how I felt both times I encountered him. How it should have been the very best experience of my life but I just felt…small…instead.

"He's a predator. I smelled it all over him. And he's messing with your head right when you need to be at the top of your game. Do you want me to go with you and tell someone? What do you want to do, Cara? I got you."

I lean forward and wrap her in a huge hug, and she pats my back.

"Well, now I got lotion on your shirt."

A laugh escapes from my throat, lightening the pressure a bit. I decide to ask Coach Lucy for advice, and Jay agrees to hold me accountable to do so.

———

The next morning, I feel both heavier and lighter as I drive us to work. I will happily admit that the yoga practice loosened up my hips a ton and I don't miss the big smiles from the coaching staff as they watch us work through our drills.

We scrimmage through a few different lineup combinations and Ben, our head coach, claps his hands as he blows a series of long blasts on his whistle. "Hot damn, gals. Who's ready to slay some Boston ballers?"

My team erupts in cheers, and he claps a few more times. "Go on and eat and get cleaned up and I'll see you in the theater for film in an hour."

He practically skips into the tunnel, and I notice the men's team filing out of their locker room, ready to take the field. I decide I want to get this over with before I see Wes again, so I hustle after the coaches to find Lucy.

I tap her on the arm, asking, "Can I talk to you for a second?"

She turns, smiling, but sees my face and her expression turns serious. "Of course, Cara. Come into my office."

I follow her and sit on the edge of the seat opposite her desk, not wanting to get sweat and grime on her nice chairs. Rather than walk around and sit in her own chair, Lucy perches on the edge of the desk, hands folded on her lap. "What's up?"

I look around her, to a picture of her family. There is a series of framed photographs on her desk of her with the men's coach, her with a little boy and a series of that same boy growing toward manhood. She's also got a wall of photos of a person who must be her daughter, looking fierce as she stares straight into the camera with dark hair and grey eyes. That woman looks like someone who would kick Lou Rubeo in the balls if he ever touched her face.

I take a deep breath. "Have you, um, ever felt ... weird ... around the staff from the national team?"

"Pah!" Lucy laughs. "Only every time I see them. Bev and Pat and Akemi are odd ducks, but I think that's what makes them so good at what they do."

I shake my head. "No. I mean, the management staff. The office guys."

Lucy frowns and grips the edge of her desk. "Did something happen, honey?"

I swallow and nod. Then I shake my head. "It might have been inadvertent? I just ... felt ... super uncomfortable when Mr. Rubeo was—"

My words leave me. It feels almost like I wet myself as a hot wave rolls over my body. Am I embarrassed, I wonder, or shamed? I don't know how to even describe what happened in a way that doesn't seem like I'm making a mountain from a mole hill.

Lucy's frown deepens. "Cara, he fails to set me at ease.

I've just always had a yucky feeling about him. You can tell me if he crossed a line. I want you to know that anything you tell me, I believe you. You are an essential part of our organization and I'm on your side."

I nod my head a few times and tears leak down my cheeks, adding to the warmth that's still flooding my body. "It was more that he just kept getting into my personal space? And then right after I saw you in the elevator in California ... he ... touched my cheek?" Her eyes harden and her nostrils flare. Lucy leans forward and grasps my hand, nodding. "He backed me up against a pole and I worried he was going to kiss me." I close my eyes as I spit out that last part. I do not add that I think he only stopped because Wes came around the corner. I certainly do not add that I'd just left Wes's bed, naked, and he thought I was preparing to jump into someone else's right away.

Lucy makes a low, angry sound and squeezes my hand gently. "Honey, that is not okay. It's not okay that you didn't feel safe or that you had to worry about someone from your place of work—because you were most certainly there for a job interview, make no mistake. Gah! I'm just so angry."

I nod rapidly, exhaling deeply as a weight lifts from my shoulders. Lucy clucks her tongue and releases my hand. "What would you like to do, Cara? Do you want me to help you file a complaint?"

"Oh. Gosh, no. I can't do that." I think about the upcoming US friendly match against Germany, how selections are meant to begin in the next few weeks. "I feel better just talking about it with you."

Lucy takes a deep breath and looks over my shoulder at the photos of her family. "You know, Cara, I have experience with that sort of man. Personal experience." Her expression hardens. "Statistically, he's not going to stop at just making you feel uncomfortable."

I swallow thickly and lean against the back of the chair for support. Lucy exhales deeply a few more times. "I'd like to make sure you're not alone in any spaces he might be. In fact, I am going to have the whole team put the buddy system into play while we're in Boston. We've got the press hounding us anyway with playoffs coming up. Everyone on the team can probably use backup."

I swallow a few more times and bend down for my bag, fumbling to try to open my water bottle. Lucy stoops to help me and rubs my back as I drink deeply. "Thank you," I tell her, my voice wavering.

"Of course, Cara. Would you like a hug?"

I nod, sinking into her embrace, listening to my stomach gurgle with the first real hunger I've experienced in weeks.

CHAPTER 5
WES

THE YOGA MUST HAVE WORKED because Uncle Hawk says I've had my best week yet. I'm still not on the travel roster, but I'm feeling better about my chances of getting there. After Sunday morning training, I walk into my Aunt Alice and Uncle Tim's house right on time for family dinner. Which means I'm the last to arrive because this family shows up early any time there's food up for grabs. I can hear the ruckus from the front porch—the sound of four Stag brothers, their wives, and whichever of the eleven Stag kids are not currently away at school.

I can also smell the feast from the front porch, the aroma of garlic and herbs making me wish I could stay here forever, maybe roll around in that scent. Aunt Alice has been working around athlete meal plans ever since Uncle Hawk played pro soccer and now all my cousins' college coaches are jealous of the lean protein and whole grain smorgasbords. She regularly photographs them to post on the teams' social media pages.

I brace myself for a record scratch silence when I step into the kitchen, brimming with my tall, athletic relatives. I sidle up to the counter and snatch a piece of shrimp cocktail from a platter, managing to get it into my mouth before my aunts smother me in hugs. "Wesley!" Alice and Aunt Juniper squeeze me from each side and Aunt Lucy tips her chin at me from where she's deep in conversation with my mom.

It takes a minute for my mom to see me and when she does, her face shifts from calm into obvious concern. "Wes," she whispers. "Come here." She holds her arms out for a hug, and I step into her embrace, not realizing how badly I missed this until her red hair is tickling my nose while I lean over her. She starts smoothing my shoulders and checking me for damage before sliding the shrimp plate toward me on the counter. "Eat, babe. Your Uncle Hawk is whittling you down to bare bones." She turns to look for my uncle, who leans against the wall, holding a beer and listening to my Uncle Ty prattle on about the ice hockey tots he coaches. "Hawk!" Mom points a finger at him. "Why is my son so thin? He needs his strength for his back."

Uncle Hawk takes a swig of his beer, glancing around the room. I don't see my dad yet, so I guess he and Uncle Tim are outside manning the grill. "Emma, your son is at top form. He's lean, agile, and he's finally got loose hips."

Mom squeezes my side, which tickles, and I twitch under her grasp. "He's too thin."

I want her to stop worrying about old injuries. I also want to mutter something about not commenting on people's bodies, which she drilled into us for years. I have vivid memories of her shaking a finger at Ricky and me, her silver life alert bracelet clinking as she spoke. But I want my parents to be cool with me more than I want to be right, so I pat her hand. "I feel great, Mom. Squeeze my bicep." I flex for her and Aunt Juniper swats me with a towel.

Mom leans back and frowns. "Your back feels great, too?" *And here we go.* My cousins Odin and Gunnar cram literal handfuls of popcorn into their mouths, snickering when they see my expression. I scratch the side of my head with my middle finger as they pass the snack bowl to our cousins Stellen and Byron.

"My back is just fine, Mom. I told you—the physical therapists know what they're doing. I followed their instructions to the letter, and it barely bothers me anymore." It's not totally a lie. Just the part about it never hurting. I've actually felt great in the week since I took that yoga class. And besides, every professional athlete has aches and pains while they're in season. I keep waiting for my uncles to back me up on this, or maybe for one of my linebacker or hockey star cousins to pipe up that they, too, have recurring pain.

"Cut the crap, son. I wrote the book on fake stories." My dad must have come in the porch door while I was talking. He stands with his tattooed arms crossed over his chest, forearms flexing as he clenches and releases his fists. "Your mother and I were there in the room after you took that hit during college playoffs, in case you forgot. The team doctor mentioned surgery and possible paralysis."

I roll my eyes and cram another shrimp in my mouth. "He absolutely did not say I'm at risk for paralysis." Mom holds up a hand, but I shake my head. "He said the surgery to repair a herniated disc can sometimes damage the spine. And then he reminded you guys that all surgery has risks." I don't want to play this card, but it's been months of this sort of treatment from my parents and I've had enough. "Was it not risky for an epileptic person to get pregnant? Twice?"

Dad shoves off the wall and strides toward me. His nostrils flare as he jabs a finger into my sternum. "Watch your mouth."

"Hey, Thatch, I'm gonna take the kids to set the table while Alice finishes up in here." Ty grabs a huge stack of plates and gestures toward my cousins, who reluctantly put down the snack bowl and pick up baskets of silverware and napkins, following my uncles into the dining room.

In the meantime, Dad steps toward my mother, who rubs

his back with her palm, tugging on her hair with her other hand. "Wesley, why would you choose that risk? A game isn't the same thing as the choice to grow a family."

I grab my own hair with both hands, the sting grounding me as I prepare to explain myself *again*. "Mom, I don't know how else to explain to you that there's nothing else that makes me happy. That soccer is my creative flow state. You write books because you said the stories scream at you to be set free, right?"

I turn to face my dad. "You blow glass because the images haunt you until you give them shape. You said that." I lean forward and grip the edge of the counter. "I feel that way about my sport. When I blow past a defender or send the perfect pass to a teammate, it's like all is right in the world for that second. The next second, I make some other sort of magic happen, together with another teammate."

I pound a fist on the counter, making Aunt Alice jump, and she backs out of the room with a plate of chicken, mouthing her apologies. Alone with my parents I let my head fall forward, closing my eyes. "I'm not going to tell you I don't worry about my back. I mean, it's my spine. I get it. But Mom, Dad...you have to let me pursue this opportunity. Do you know how few people are capable of playing professional sports?" Dad opens his mouth to talk but I straighten up and charge ahead. "Maybe I only get a year of this. Maybe I never get to start in a game. But I have to try. I have to give every-thing while I can and trust that you've given me the tools I need to figure out the next steps when we get there."

Dad swallows, his throat bobbing underneath his trimmed beard that's got streaks of white sprouting up throughout. Mom clutches his hand. "Wesley, it's not easy for parents to forget the sight of their child crying in pain."

I nod. "I know that, Mom. I know. And just like you asked your parents, I'm asking you to trust me with my own body. I'm asking you not to put me in a glass cage." I look my father right in the eye. "You always told Mom she can do anything, that you'd be right by her side if she needed help. Well, now I need you cheering for me."

I don't give them a chance to respond. I'm not actually ready to discuss this further, so I walk past them into the dining room and grab a chair at the far end of the table, in between a few of my cousins. The massive crew has already decimated the platters of food my aunt prepared, and I have to fight through elbows to fill my plate. I eat quietly, looking around the table at my family, who mercifully ignores me while they talk about the non-soccer pro sports teams here in the city.

Uncle Ty's former hockey team, the Fury, haven't won a cup in years and my cousins all get heated as they talk about the pre-season exhibition games being played in Australia this year.

I'm glad for the comfort of the banter, the emphatic analysis, and the way my cousins tease each other about their predictions. And then I see my Aunt Lucy looking as miserable as I feel and wonder what else is going on. From everything I've seen and heard, the women's team has been crushing it on the field, so I have no idea why my aunt's face looks so tense as she talks to my uncle. He grips her leg under the table, nodding, before he leans back and scratches his chin.

Aunt Alice stands, then, and asks the kids to clear the table, even though the youngest kids here are twenty years old. This invites a mass eruption of dessert predictions from among her own offspring. My uncles, aunts, and parents all wander into the living room with their wine glasses.

I shouldn't drink alcohol during the season, especially when I'm working so hard to secure a starting spot on the team, but I snatch an empty glass from the table and walk up behind my Aunt Lucy, who has a bottle of white tucked under her arm. "Hey." I gesture for the bottle, and she frowns at me. "I'm having half a glass. Are you my aunt today or a member of the management team at work?"

She tips the bottle and pours me a few mouthfuls of wine, arching her brow before she brings the entire bottle to her lips and takes a deep swig.

"Woah. Can I ask what's got you so upset? You're not usually a big drinker, Aunt Luce."

She sighs and wipes her mouth with the back of her hand. "Cara Moreno and Jay Whittaker got tapped for the national team after our match with Boston the other day."

My eyes fly wide, and it feels like my eyebrows will disappear into my hair. Why the hell was Cara upset at yoga if she made the national team? "Um, that's phenomenal. Isn't it?"

Lucy nods. "Yes. Absolutely." She flashes a forced smile and takes her wine to the back porch, where she gestures wildly at my Uncle Hawk. I swallow the tiny portion of wine in my glass. It tingles in my mouth. I haven't had anything outside my meal plan since … I close my eyes against the memory of gorging on breadsticks and cheese pasta in bed with Cara at the tryout camp in California a few months back. We both decided to indulge in between rounds of the most explosive, intense sex of my life.

Lost in my memories, I don't hear my Uncle Tim talking to me until he snaps his fingers in front of my face. "Wes? Hello?"

I shake my head. "Sorry. What was that?"

He rattles a blue recycling bin at me. "I asked if you could go out back and dump that by the garage."

"Oh." I set my empty glass on the counter. "Sure. Sorry."

He grunts and grabs a sponge to scrub off the counters and I make my way down the basement steps and out the back door. I don't intend to eavesdrop on Hawk and Lucy, still arguing on the deck above me. But they're pretty loud.

"…what do they expect me to do, Hawk? The man made her uncomfortable enough that she said something to me.

That speaks volumes." My aunt's voice cracks and I hear her gulping wine. I pause in place, resting the bin of recycling against the wall. If I dump it now, the rattling cans will alert them, and they'll stop talking...so I guess I'm actively rubbernecking on Lucy's drama at this point.

Uncle Hawk's voice is low, and I know he's trying to soothe her. "You have to be up front about it. Talk to the player rep, at least, or someone from Tim's legal team."

My aunt scoffs. "Like Tim ever handled anything quietly."

"Lucy, do you really want this kept quiet? Cara Moreno is more important to the organization than some guy in a suit with a desk job."

I'm so startled to hear Cara's name that I drop the bin and, as predicted, my aunt and uncle stop talking. Hawk leans over the deck rail to ask, "Everything okay down there? Oh. Hey, Wes."

I wave a hand. "Just dumping recycling for Uncle Tim."

Lucy frowns. "Better get inside for cookies before your cousins take them all. Alice used the monk fruit sweetener this time. Whatever that means."

I smile at her. I'd wrinkle my nose at whole grain cookies with odd-sounding ingredients if I didn't know from experience that those fuckers are going to be damn delicious, despite being packed with spirulina.

I head inside, back up to the kitchen, trying to make sense of why Aunt Lucy would be talking about Cara. Aunt Lucy mentioned a sticky situation with the national staff, and I remember Lou Rubeo all cozy with Cara in the hall in California. And then Cara cried as we argued after yoga.

A tingle of doubt skitters through my gut as I think of Aunt Lucy's concerned face, at the way she sounded so tortured when talking to my uncle. What did she mean, Cara was uncomfortable? I'm about to grab a cookie when something else about that trip sparks hesitation, a hiccup in my gut.

What if Rubeo was a predator instead of Cara seeking out

that kind of attention? The president of Soccer USA making a pass at one of Lucy's players would definitely be the sort of thing that would set my aunt on edge.

I think back to the moment I lost Cara, to that vision of her in the hall with Rubeo. I walked around the corner to see him leaning in toward her, suggestively. I saw his finger tracing a line down her cheek. But what did her body language convey? I can't even remember. My memory only picks back up from the moment her eyes met mine and I almost let her see how much it stung to have been left.

I realize with staggering, horrifying clarity that I misjudged her. That she's been trying to tell me for weeks that something terrible happened and all I did was ghost her and leave her alone to deal with the effects of a slime ball making her feel unsafe. I've been swimming through a haze of hurt feelings that I wanted something more with a woman who walked out on me … only to realize I fucked everything up beyond recognition.

"I have to go." I blurt this declaration loud enough that Mom hears. She makes her way toward me through the throng of Stags, but I don't stop to hug her. I have to find Cara and apologize.

I dash out the front door as my father hollers for me to come back, but all I can think about is making amends.

CHAPTER 6
CARA

"I JUST DON'T KNOW what you want me to say, Cara."
Mama sounds like I interrupted her with something frivolous
when I called her and Papi to tell them I got chosen to represent our country in a friendly match against Germany.
They've been divorced for years, but we always do a three-
way call for these weekly chats. Apparently so they can
present a united front that I'm still and forever doing it
wrong.

"Mama, really? You can't say, 'Felicidades, Cara! I'm so
proud of you?'"

She sniffs.

Papi makes a humming sound. "And they're paying you a
salary to play football like the men?"

"Yes, Papi. God, I've been explaining this to you for
months. And I'm not playing *like* the men. I play women's
football. I'm a professional athlete."

"Watch your language, Cara." He snaps a reprimand like
I'm still a child. And maybe it's childish to expect them to
understand after all this time.

"We just want you to think about your future. What about
starting a family? Having babies?"

"Yes." Papi chimes in with his machismo opinions. "These footballers earn millions. Messi is in Miami earning $50 million. Your cousin saw him at Costco."

I roll my eyes, glad they can't see me doing so to find another thing to chastise me about. "Messi is married with kids."

"And you're earning millions, yes?"

"Papi, you know I'm not."

"Mm hmm. Well, a man don't like a woman who earns more than him anyway."

"Luis, that's not true and you know it." I know better than to hope my mother is on my side with this interjection. She starts listing telenovela starlets with "ordinary" husbands and would continue for hours if I didn't cut her off.

"I'm not playing soccer to find a husband. I'm playing soccer because I love it and I love this freaking country and I thought you'd be proud that I will be representing it."

"Such language. Is that what they teach you at these schools with the men and women in class together? Is that how you talk to people in Pittsburgh? What does your priest say?"

I dig a knuckle into my temple with the hand not holding the phone, trying to decide what to say next. A knock at the door catches me off guard and I glance down the hall. Jay is out on a date with a woman who asked for her autograph after our last home game, so I worry that she forgot her key or something. "Mama, Papi, I need to go. Someone is at the door."

"Just think about what I said, Cara. You can still come back and find a job here in Findlay."

"Mami, I appreciate that. I will call you soon, okay." I hang up and throw the phone on the sofa, muttering to myself about my contract, feeling thankful that I have at least three years here in Pittsburgh where most people seem to understand that women have other goals in life than making babies.

Whoever's at the door knocks again, hesitantly, and I shuffle over to the peep hole. I gasp audibly when I see Wes Stag on the other side of the door.

"Cara, I came to apologize," he says as I press my back against the door, one hand to my chest as if I could still the racing heart inside my ribs. "Can I please come in and talk to you? I brought you something."

I should tell him to get lost. I should ignore him and hide in my room, ghost him like he did to me. He was so mean and dismissive when I tried to talk with him after yoga. For some reason I lean to the side and look through the peep hole again. Wes has one arm above his head, leaning on the door, face close to the little lens. His eyes seem sincere.

I sigh and open the door and melt a bit when his face shifts into a grin, like he's happy to see me. He holds out his hand, displaying a bright blue cube. "I brought you a power adapter." I arch a brow in confusion. His grin widens. "For when you're in France, with the national team. So you can charge your phone and stuff…"

I blink at him, unsteady on my feet. How does he know I got selected? How is it that this man who doesn't even like me understands the significance of my achievement so much that he bought me the perfect celebration gift? "Thank you," I whisper, accepting the cube and turning it over in my hand.

Wes points at the adapter. "There are different plug configurations depending on where you're going. See here? I guess the outlets are shaped different in Australia compared to Europe." He smiles at me, expectantly. Waiting. I look between him and the cube, unsure what to do. "So, can I come in and apologize now?"

I shake myself back to the present moment. "Yes. Sorry. Um, do you want something to drink?" I groan, embarrassed that I'm offering hospitality and my own apologies to someone who already said he came here to offer me those things. "We can sit on the couch."

Jay and I don't have a dining table. We eat at the counter, where we have four high stools, two of which are piled with clean laundry yet to be sorted and put away. The small table in the entryway is currently covered in mail and canned tuna —just a few of the side effects from a series of away matches.

Wes seems not to notice and walks to the couch, easing his long torso into the corner. He places his hands on his thighs and waits for me to join him. I pluck my phone from the other corner of the couch and set it on the end table, turning my body to face Wes.

"You seem frazzled," he starts. "Is this a bad time?"

I shake my head. "You know, just dealing with parents who don't understand why I'd want to play professional sports."

"Ah." He nods knowingly. "I know a few things about that." He swallows and rubs his palms along his jeans. I try not to think about the thighs I know hide beneath that dark denim. "So, I overheard my Aunt Lucy today at dinner."

I wrinkle my nose. "Should I know who that is?"

His brows shoot up and he stiffens. "Lucy Moyer? Your assistant coach?"

I tap my fingers and squint. "Coach Lucy is related to you?"

Wes barks out a laugh. "It's so refreshing when people don't know my whole family history." He shakes his head, smiling. "Hawk Moyer, the men's team coach, is my dad's brother. He's married to Lucy." My mouth forms an "oh" of surprise. "You can imagine the mind fuck it creates for me when I'm trying to prove myself and people think I just made this team because of my family."

"I … had no idea."

He waves a hand in the air. "So, my Uncle Ty played pro

hockey, too. And my dad and Uncle Tim are lifelong runners. All us kids—there are 11 of us all together—all of us are athletic whether we like it or not. Many of us are playing D1 sports in college or putting ourselves out there for the pros. My cousin Odin is probably going to play in the NFL."

"Wow. Well, you know my family doesn't believe real women play sports."

Wes extends a hand like he wants to touch me but changes his mind and drapes it over the back of the couch. "Let me know their address and I'll have my Aunt Juniper send them a picture of her Olympic medal hanging in her judge's chambers at the courthouse downtown."

I chuckle, imagining my parents not knowing what to make of such a passive aggressive package. But then I don't know what else to say. "Um, you said you were going to apologize?"

He nods and licks his lips. "I don't know where to start so I'm just going to dive into it." I nod and swallow. Feeling exposed, I grab a throw pillow and clutch it to my chest. "I fucked up, Cara. I saw you and Mr. Rubeo standing together in the hall and I assumed the worst of you when I should have seen the worst in him."

I inhale a shaky breath through my nose and tears well up in my eyes as Wes brings up Lou Rubeo.

"My aunt didn't mention anything specific—she had no idea I was lurking nearby, anyway. But she said something at family dinner about there being issues with the staff on the national team. And, well, I couldn't help but remember how upset you were after yoga." He drags a hand through his hair and squeezes his eyes shut. "God, Cara, I'm just so damn sorry. I should have trusted you...I should have trusted what we shared together. Instead, I just made everything worse."

I close my eyes and a single tear rolls down my face. "I really felt a connection with you in California."

He slumps further into the couch, his proud shoulders

sagging. "I felt it too, Cara. Like nothing I ever felt before. I'm embarrassed that I ruined that."

The air is thick with regret, and I want to tell him it's okay, that we can pick up where we left off...but he hurt me. His actions and his words...and lack of words...it hurt me. I'm already dealing with enough rejection from my parents plus navigating the delicate situation with the national team, when the flipping president of the organization makes me want to vomit. "I appreciate you coming here to apologize," I manage to tell him. I take a deep breath and release the pillow long enough to tuck my hair behind my ears.

He smiles and reaches out a hand to finger the end of my ponytail. I accept his touch, missing the contact I once savored with him. "I also came to congratulate you. I'm proud of you for making the cut." A beam of light expands inside my chest at his words, at his recognition of me achieving a lifelong dream. "When do you leave for training camp?"

I hug the pillow again, this time in excitement. "Not until later. National camp isn't supposed to conflict with league play, but we made the playoffs ... as you know."

Wes's smile is even larger now and he leans one elbow on the arm of the couch, grinning. "Of course, I know. I'm vying for field time in our own playoff run myself."

I laugh, sinking happily into comfortable conversation with this man, who understands my work, my ambition. Even if he was a dick about it, he found a really thoughtful way to apologize. "I'd love to come to a game and see you play, Wes. If it works out."

His sneaker taps on the floor, and he shifts his posture, bringing his body just a bit closer to mine. "We could look at our travel schedules...see if that will work out anytime soon? I want to see you play, too." His smile would melt the ice off the sides of our freezer—and it's got quite a lot of buildup since Jay and I haven't been here to keep up with monitoring it.

"We can do that." I grab my phone and pull up my calendar, and he does the same.

CHAPTER 7
WES

MY NAME IS on the roster as a sub for the Forge game against Charleston. Not a starter, yet, but this is the first time I'll be eligible to take the field as a professional athlete. I should feel an irresistible urge to call my family with this news, especially since I want to get to them before my uncle blabs. But when I see the roster posted by the showers, my first thought is to tell Cara.

It's only been a few days since I made amends, but we've been texting back and forth. She's going to be able to watch my game this weekend, since the Hot Metal plays Charleston's women's team the same day. The women play first, though, so I'll be warming up and unable to watch her play.

I hurry and change into my sweats and shoot her a text message.

> Call me after your practice? I've got news.

"Wes, got a second?" My uncle pokes his head out from his office and I nod, sliding the phone in my pocket as I walk toward him. "Shut the door, kid." I do, and then my uncle beams and claps his hands slowly. "I couldn't be any more proud of you if you were my own son, Wesley. You really stepped up your game the last week or so, bud."

He tousles my wet hair and I bat his arm away. "Ah, knock it off, Uncle Hawk. And thank you. I've been working hard."

He leans against the edge of his desk, arms crossed over his chest. "Have you talked to your parents any more since dinner at Tim's?"

I shake my head. "We'll work it out eventually. I do wish they could come see me play. I wonder if my coach knows whether I'll actually get any time on the field..."

"Do you want me to be your uncle right now or your coach?" He winks at me, then smooths a hand along his chin. "I don't really see Thatcher and Emma traveling for this one, though. I think it's parents' weekend at your brother's school."

I shrug. "All the more reason to keep working for a start in a home match, right?"

"That's the attitude." He claps me on the back and then pulls me in tight for a hug. "All right, I stink. Get out so I can shower."

I laugh and head toward the parking lot, checking my phone. I grin entirely too hard when I see a text from Cara, even if it is just a thumbs up emoji. I know she's feeling tender after how I treated her. This isn't like California where we were both immediately on the same page about being majorly into one another. If I ever want her to be mine again, I'm going to have to work as hard with her as I will on the field for that starring role.

I decide to hit up Costco and because I'm a good Stag who thinks of the herd, I text my cousins to see if anyone needs anything.

YOUNG STAG GROUP CHAT

Who needs ten pounds of Doritos?

WYATT:

You're not really going to eat that crap in season are you?

ODIN:

I will always eat Doritos. And a few pounds of beef jerky, please

PETEY:

I'm going to silence this thread for awhile since I doubt you're going to deliver to me in Ithaca.

STELLEN:

Always bragging about that Ivy League education...

Wes, I'll take cheese sticks.

Which kind?

STELLEN:

All the kinds. I don't care. Surprise me.

GUNNAR:

Better toss in a bucket of dairy pills if Stelly is going to be pounding cheese in the apartment.

STELLEN:

Fuck you, Gun. I'm going to fart on your pillow right now while you're at class.

They carry on this way while I drive to the store and fill a massive cart with snack food, most of it healthy. I'm about to check out when I wheel the cart past the pasta aisle and notice an end cap with bouquets of fresh flowers. Do I want to be a guy who buys a woman flowers, and maybe pays a custodian to slip them in her locker for me?

I check my watch and it's barely three. I still have plenty of time before rush hour traffic makes this plan ridiculous.

The bouquets are only $9, so I toss one on top of the cart before I can change my mind. Only, when I get back to the stadium, I don't need to find someone to infiltrate the women's locker room for me because I spy Cara walking out the side gate with her roommate.

I throw my Jeep in park and leap out with the flowers. "Hey, Cara," I shout as I jog toward her, realizing I must look ridiculous or frantic or both.

She turns toward my voice and then sees the flowers. She tilts her head to the side, confused.

Her roommate looks at the flowers and then into my face and squints. "I'll see you at home, Cara. I gotta go."

"Wait," Cara shouts. "We rode in together."

"What?" Jay holds a hand over one ear. "I can't hear you over the train. Sorry, gotta go. Bye."

I make a silent note to buy Jay something nice for meddling on my behalf. I grin and put one hand in my pocket, holding the flowers out toward Cara with the other. She looks around as her teammates file out of the stadium, heads bent and talking to one another. I get the sense Cara doesn't want people at work to see her getting flowers from someone on the men's team, so I step behind a brick column and gesture for her to come closer. I choose not to believe she's feeling awkward about getting flowers from me specifically.

"What're these for, Wes?" She bites her lip and looks down at the bouquet again like it's some massive gesture and not a grocery store bunch of flowers.

"Well, I thought of you when I saw them. So I bought them."

She smiles, like she's trying not to but can't help it. The tiny pull at the corners of her mouth does something to my heart rate. I love knowing I made her smile. Half-smile. "Is that what you wanted to talk about? I was about to call you when you shouted my name!"

I shake my head and shake the flowers until she takes them from me, sniffing the bouquet. "Nah, these are separate. I wanted to tell you I made the sub roster. For Charleston."

"Wes! That's outstanding!" Her entire face lights up and I can tell that she means it, that she's truly happy for me.

"Would you want to celebrate with me?" I'm operating totally off book here, utterly astonishing myself as these ideas fly into my head and a little too invested in her response to me putting myself out there. "I'd love to buy you an herbal tea. Plus, you know, I hear you need a ride."

She laughs and I know she's aware there isn't much we can eat or drink at a restaurant leading up to a game, not with our nutrition plans. "That sounds nice, Wes. Thank you."

I gesture toward my car, stopped haphazardly. Cara laughs as she sees some women from the Hot Metal swerving around my Jeep on their way out of the stadium parking lot. "I think we'd better get a move on since you're causing a traffic jam."

She sniffs the orange and pink flowers and I keep my distance, even though I'd love to put an arm around her. Smell her hair, tell her that I think talking things out with her opened me up more than the yoga class did and really let me shine this week to earn this spot.

I unlock the car and lean past Cara to open her door, but she's already flung open the back door to toss her bag inside. Her nose wrinkles and she looks around at all the boxes in the car. "What's that smell?"

"Oh, god. Sorry about that." I lean past her and shove the boxes to make room for her bag. I do notice that Cara sets the flowers gingerly on top, out of harm's way. I smile and explain, "My cousins wanted seaweed snacks and beef jerky. I think we're getting some sort of chemical reaction from the paired odors."

Her head flies back as she laughs. "Have you tasted those

seaweed things before? My one roommate used to love them."

I shake my head and accept that I'm not going to be able to open the door for her as Cara slides past me and into the passenger seat. "They taste like a fart. And they give you *horrible* breath."

"Note to self: do not eat seaweed snacks near Cara."

She buckles her seatbelt and leans an elbow on the window, turning her body toward mine while I drive. "Don't avoid them on my account. You need your iron to play for the Forge."

"Are we making metal jokes now? Hot metal jokes?"

"Okay, okay. Enough Steel City puns." She taps her fingers on her legs in time with the music over the radio. I head up Forbes Avenue toward the Oakland neighborhood where four of my cousins share a college apartment. There's a tea shop nearby.

"Is it okay if I stop quick and unload all this cheese and stuff? I have a key to my cousins' place, so it'll be quick."

"That's fine. Are we talking about cousins like *actual* cousins or like how every Latino family friend is my auntie and their kids are my cousins?"

"Oh, these are my actual cousins. My dad is one of four, and each brother has … a lot of kids." I put on my turn signal to head down Atwood Street toward the university-owned apartment building where a lot of athletes live, including my extended family. I parallel park in a loading zone by the fire station across the street and hop out, filling my arms with an awkward stack of boxes. I'm about to tell Cara that I'll be right back for the rest of it when I notice her standing beside me, arms laden with jerky and chips.

"Lead the way," she grins, and I marvel at how in sync we are, even now when our friendship still has an undercurrent of hesitation. I shake away the thought and hurry toward my cousins' apartment. But then I realize I don't have a spare hand to get the key from my pants pocket. I'm in the middle of an awkward maneuver to rest the boxes against the wall and pull my hand free, when Cara says, "Here. I got it." Before I can say a word, she slides her hand into my sweats and plucks out the keychain.

I grow immediately, achingly hard at the heat of her touch, at the memory and familiarity of her body near mine. I draw in a shaky breath, worried I might actually come in my pants like a teenager. "Which one is it?" Cara shakes the keys, questioning, and I shake myself back to reality.

"The one with the purple ring," I manage to choke out. Cara unlocks the door and holds it open for me. I drop the boxes just past the threshold and gesture for her to do the same with her armload.

"Shouldn't we put the cheese in the fridge? I don't want it to go bad." I'm well aware that any lingering here could lead to a cousin returning from class, or waking up from a nap, and I'm not ready to subject Cara to the Stag family brand of inquisition. She already knows my aunt and uncle and I tell myself I don't want to impact any professional boundaries she's established at work.

She's on her way back from the kitchen before I can tell her the cheese is fine for a few hours. Beaming, she walks past me into the hall, and I lock the door behind us as I follow her. "That's so nice of you to take them supplies, Wes. I never had a big family like that."

"You're an only child, right?"

"Mm hmm. I have relative-cousins in Florida, and like I said, I have 'cousins' near home … but they wouldn't exactly drive to my college apartment with care packages."

I swallow, remembering the tension with her parents and their outdated views on women in sports. "It helps that we all live close by, I'm sure."

"Well, anyway, I think it's nice." Cara once again gets herself inside my Jeep before I can open the door for her, and

I'm left on the curb looking weird as I watch her buckle her seatbelt.

The tea shop ends up not having seating, which leads to me driving Cara home and sitting on her balcony in a camp chair. She's got a sweet view of the Allegheny River, and we sip our drinks as we watch people rowing crew and kayaking. She smiles at the water. "Is it weird that I love watching the water sports? It just looks so peaceful, somehow."

I slurp my tea. "Not weird at all. I think I told you my Aunt Juniper rowed crew in the Olympics. All of us took rowing lessons from her."

"That's so cool."

I shake my head. "It looks cool, maybe, but those people are masochists. Nothing has ever burned my lungs more than Aunt June barking me through a power 20."

Cara laughs and leans forward on the rail, the breeze blowing her curls around. "What about the kayaks, then? Are those harder than they look?"

I swallow the urge to make a joke about things looking hard, but I can tell Cara catches her slip because she lifts her eyebrows as she slurps the rest of her iced tea. There's a weighted pause where we just look at one another. I want so many things … to kiss her and hold her, to shout over the balcony that I got called up to the roster.

I'm about to tell her I need to quit while I'm ahead, make an excuse and head home, but her roommate starts shouting from the living room.

"Cara! We got our workout schedules from Akemi. You're gonna want to go to bed immediately and rest up." Cara smiles knowingly, and I can imagine exactly what she's thinking. She's got that dread of how hard it will be on top of her Hot Metal workouts, plus the simmering burn to demolish the benchmarks. I remind myself that work has to come first for her, and it should be that way for me, too. We both have too much to prove to get lost in flirtation.

"I get it," I tell her, my voice softer than I intended. "I'll let you get your rest. Sounds like you need it."

"See you at work, Stag." She grins and crunches an ice cube from her glass, and I actually experience a pang of jealousy from a frozen shard of water.

"See you at work."

CHAPTER 8
CARA

I'M NOT sure how Wesley Stag and I transition from an herbal tea hangout to making each other lunch on alternating days, but all week, I've been prepping turkey wraps and slicing carrots into intricate shapes, constantly trying to up my lunch game before I meet him outside the stadium in between drills and film and his physical therapy. We eat by the river unless it's raining, watching the barges chug past and waving at the occasional morning booze cruise.

Yesterday, he handed me a joke lunch full of that seaweed stuff, so today I disguised a turkey meatloaf to look like a cupcake, topped with riced cauliflower frosting and chive sprinkles. I hand him the container and bat my eyes, awaiting his response. Despite my hesitation around him and my anxiety that he'll ditch me again at the first sign of trouble, I'm growing addicted to the way I feel when I'm around Wes.

"Dessert for lunch? You're pretty confident in yourself now that you're on the national team roster, Moreno." He winks and sniffs the food. His brow furrows. "What is this?"

"I promise it meets our dietary parameters." I shift my posture so I'm leaning forward with my elbows on my knees, my own meatloaf container still sealed since I didn't decorate mine any special way.

"Did you call my Aunt Alice or something?"

"You know I have no idea who your relatives are, Stag. Try it!"

Wes wrinkles his nose, shrugs, and takes a bite of the cupcake. I watch his face shift as he tastes the savory food when he was expecting sweet. I laugh as he moves through shock and into acceptance and actual enjoyment. My meatloaf is damn tasty, thank you very much. "Id dis meatloaf?" Wes covers his mouth with his free hand as he chews.

I nod and take a bite of my own dish, feeling nostalgia when the taste of oregano with a touch of cumin hits my tongue. I swallow my bite and explain, "I used black beans to bind it all since I know you're off rice right now."

"I love it. I'm not going to be able to beat this. What did you use for the sprinkles?"

I shrug and nudge him with my shoulder. "Are you admitting defeat? Is the great Wesley Stag giving up and naming me lunch-making champion?"

"Nah. Not really. Besides, I have a few days to figure it out since we travel tomorrow, right?"

I nod and enjoy the shiver rolling through my body. I'm excited for this away game. "Coach Akemi will be in Charleston watching."

He smiles wistfully. "I wish I could watch your game, too."

"I know you do. But I'm also excited to see yours. Jay and some of the Hot Metal are going to stick around for at least the first half."

"How generous."

"Hey, come on. How many of your teammates can name a player on my team?"

"Fair point." Wes finishes his cupcake and takes a deep pull from his water bottle. He fidgets with the cap and stares out at the water for a bit. "Are you doing anything tonight?" I hesitate just long enough that Wes quickly adds, "I was planning to watch a game and wondered if you wanted to join me."

A flurry of emotion whirls inside me at the prospect of alone time with Wes. Will we touch? Will I be able to recover if we don't? This man and I have an electric connection when he's not snapping to conclusions. I'm not sure how to navigate that, and I'm not sure how much I can let it distract me from my career right now. "What game? Whose house?"

He taps his lips and I can tell he knows his answer will determine a lot. "How about your house if Jay doesn't mind my presence? And … maybe the last World Cup final?"

"I'll see you around six." I stand and brush the crumbs from my lap, gathering up my stuff so I can head back inside for my strategy session. Wes follows and I notice a slight wince as he stoops to grab his bag.

———

He knocks on my apartment door at 5:59 and I point finger guns at Jay, who insisted he was one of those guys who viewed time as a social construct. "Whatever, Cara. He better have food with him."

She opens the front door to reveal a long pair of legs in grey sweats, topped with a stack of takeout boxes that hide the chest and face of our visitor. "Did someone request food?" Wes bends his head to the side of the stack and grins. I force myself to look away from the sweatpants. Jay grabs the top few boxes so Wes can see where he's going, and they spread stuff out on the counter while I run around grabbing plates and silverware from the dishwasher.

"Wow, I didn't know you were bringing an entire feast."

He shrugs. "Three professional athletes can put away a lot of calories, right?" He points to the boxes. "These are actually from my Aunt Alice—the chef I was telling you about. She knew I'd be missing family dinner on Sunday, so she dropped off a huge care package."

"Wes, you didn't have to bring us your special family food." I try to imagine a circumstance where I'd share ropa vieja if my aunt sent me some from Miami.

"Shut up, Cara. I want the chef food." Jay is already digging into a container of grilled chicken and zucchini.

Wes slides a box toward me and my mouth waters at the smell of mustard and garlic. "It's really fine. You have to remember, my entire family lives within a few miles. If Aunt Alice knew Jay was craving this sort of thing, she'd probably start delivering weekly."

"I'm not gonna say no to dat." Jay squeezes her eyes shut in bliss as she devours the savory food.

"Are you watching the Lionesses game with us, Jay?" I arch a brow at her because she told me she wasn't sticking around.

"Lionesses?" Wes squints around a mouth of broccoli.

"England? World Cup final?" I wash down an incredible mouthful with a swig of water.

Wes puffs out a laugh. "I thought we were watching France versus Argentina."

Jay grins and claps us each on the back. "As much as I'd enjoy watching you two figure out that you have to specify which World Cup you meant since there's one for each gender…I'm going to watch the Seattle versus Louisville game with the other keepers." She strides toward the door and glances back over her shoulder. "In case you weren't sure, we will be watching women play soccer." Jay's cackle echoes down the hall as she leaves, and I frown at Wes.

"Do we really have to watch men's soccer?"

"Are men so gross?" He winks at me and takes a final bite of food, wiping at his mouth with a napkin.

I ball up my napkin and throw it at him. "Sometimes,

yeah. But I want to watch the women's final from last year and assess the competition."

Wes's eyes dart to the couch, where the remote lies on one of the cushions. Before I can react, he dives over the back of the couch, one long arm extended toward his goal.

"Oh, definitely not, Stag." I spring over the side of the couch. He jumped first, but I'm closer and my fingers wrap around the end with enough time to spare for me to smash the power button. "Ha."

Wes hauls both legs over the couch and under his body, using his leverage to wrestle the remote from my hands. He smashes the voice control button and shouts "show me Messi versus Mbappé."

"Don't you dare," I yell at the television in vain as the Argentinian and French flags appear on the screen. I elbow Wes in the side and lean over his lap, digging a nail into the microphone icon on the remote. "I want Spain versus England."

The screen flickers and … a random international men's game appears. Wes and I both deflate, and he groans. "I get it, Moreno. I'm sorry. Even the robots think men's soccer is the default."

I want to say something in response. I want to curse the patriarchy. But my chest is heaving, and my face is a few inches from the bulge in the center of Wes's sweatpants and all thought seeps out of my skull. Gingerly, I sit up and nestle into the corner of the couch, relinquishing the remote as Wes pulls up the women's final match.

"God, this is a good game," he whispers a few minutes in as we both adjust ourselves to the far ends of the couch. He pauses a few times to point at the screen, and I smile, appreciating his commentary. By half-time, we're an inch apart from one another on the couch, staring at the screen and barely blinking, even though we both know the outcome of the game. England gets a yellow card soon after and Wes nearly punches a hole in my coffee table as he shouts at the referee on the screen.

"Easy there, big guy." I rub a palm on his back, realizing as I do that it's probably a bad idea, but not caring enough to pull back my hand. Wes turns his head to smile at me—a warm, full-faced expression with teeth and twinkling eyes—and my heart stops a little bit. More than half of me wants to dive into him and finish what we started in California. My skin tingles just thinking about it, with my hand resting on his ribcage. Breathless, I lean back against the couch as the game continues on the television.

Wes relaxes his posture as well and soon I feel the warmth of his arm around the back of the cushions. By the time the game ends, I've got my head on his shoulder as his fingers draw gentle circles on my shoulder.

CHAPTER 9
CARA

THE WOMEN'S team flies separately from the men's team for our Charleston match. Jay grumbles about our connection in Baltimore since, based on the flight board at the airport, it seems like the men flew direct. "It's all the little shit like this that just fills me with a boiling rage sometimes, you know?" She kicks a trash can in the security line.

"Trust me, I get it. I grew up in a family where the men actually sit at the dinner table waiting to be served plates of food." Even though we do all get security pre-check as a job perk, there are so many of us that our line moves just as slowly as the regular security line. "How close are we to booking a full flight, just us? If we paired up with the men, I bet we'd be close."

Jay leans in for a retina scan and sniffs. "With the athletic trainers, I bet you're right. Just makes me hate the national office suits even more, if they think stuff like this is equitable."

Her mention of the national staff has me reflexively tightening my stomach. I'm grateful for the distraction of the x-ray machine. Once our team is through the checkpoint, we pile into the shuttle to the terminal. I see Coach Lucy talking heatedly to Coach Ben and a pang of discomfort washes over me. Is it my anxiety that leads me to suspect their disagreement is related to Lou Rubeo? They could just as easily be arguing about our starting lineup.

Once we're near our gate, Lucy peels off from the group to make a phone call. I don't mean to eavesdrop, but her voice rises as I approach. "Hey, babe. Yeah, he's going to be there … I haven't decided yet … Yeah, I know your brother can support me, but I'd like to avoid bringing a lawyer to a press conference if I can help it."

I slow my pace as much as I can without seeming obvious, and I spend both legs of our flight trying to calm my stomach, worrying that opening up to Coach Lucy created problems for the entire Pittsburgh soccer franchise.

Jay and I split up at the hotel in Charleston—each of us is rooming with someone else who plays our position—and while I like my fellow mid-fielder just fine, I don't know her well enough to open up about my off-field worries. As a result, I take the field Saturday morning with a whole suitcase of unprocessed emotional baggage.

I can't quite chase away the blockage. It's like a fog at the periphery of my vision throughout the game and I keep getting elbowed by defenders. My footwork is sloppy, and I bobble the ball a few times.

At one point I move to receive a clearing kick from Jay, but instead of cradling the ball gently to the ground so I can run with it, I lock my ankle and it bounces wildly from my foot straight to the feet of Charleston's best striker.

Worse, I freeze in shock over my mistake instead of tearing down the field after her. She weaves through our defensive line, plants her foot, and kicks the ball into the top corner of the net, past Jay's fingers. Ben subs me out with 20 minutes left in the match and I don't even question it. I slump into the sideline shelter, staring at the field and hoping my replacement has her shit together enough to turn the tide. She doesn't, and the ref whistles for the end of the game.

Coach Ben sighs and heads over to shake hands with the opposing coach. He turns back to face us. "Tough one, folks." Ben gestures his head toward the tunnel and everyone shuffles toward the locker room for our post-match meeting. I start to follow and I feel a hand on my shoulder.

"Hey, Cara, you okay?" Coach Lucy offers me a cup of hydration drink, which I accept with a shrug. She offers a watery smile. "You seemed distracted on the field. Want to talk about it?"

I shake my head, still staring ahead. I hear her inhale, hesitate, exhale. "I want to follow up with you about our conversation in my office. I want you to know that I took it very seriously, but as you know it's a very complicated situation."

"Ha." The sound puffs out of me, and I turn my head to face her, finally. She smiles as we lean against the wall in the tunnel.

"I'm sure you know the national team staff is here tonight. I meant what I said in the locker room about sticking with a buddy. One thing we know about these types of men is they behave differently with an audience."

I drain the rest of the liquid in the cup, crumple it, and toss it toward the wastebasket. I mutter my thanks to Coach Lucy, and walk toward the rest of the team in the locker room.

———

It's hard to drum up enthusiasm from my teammates to watch the men's game after our loss on the pitch. "I'm going no matter what," I say, toweling my hair after my shower. I know I'm just a rookie who came on board late season, so I'm not surprised when Jay is the only Hot Metal player to join me in the bleachers as the men take the field.

"Think anyone would notice if I ate an entire funnel cake?" She sniffs toward the concession stands longingly.

"Don't do it! You'll hate yourself in the morning. Besides, it was my fault that striker got the ball to begin with."

Jay flicks me in the shoulder. "We have four perfectly good defenders on our team who could have stopped her. Plus, you know, me."

"What's your point?" I spy Wes in the group of gold jerseys and my heart flutters a little, the first semi-joyful emotion I've felt in a few days.

"My point is that we should all be jointly eating funnel cake as a coping mechanism because we are all to blame for that loss. Not just you taking on the responsibility. Is that the reindeer?"

I squint to make sure, because a lot of the guys look the same from this distance. "Wow. He's starting. I thought he was a sub."

"Good for him." Jay claps and puts two fingers in her mouth, whistling. Ordinarily I'd call my Midfield Mamis to decompress, or at least vent-text them while I watch, but if Wes is starting, I want to pay attention.

I smile as the ref blows the whistle and the Forge center kicks the ball to Wes. I can't make out his facial expression from here, but I suspect he flashes a cocky grin to the Charleston player as Wes pulls the ball back and spins away, streaking up the right sideline with his teammates in fast support. Wes drives all the way to the top corner before sending the ball right in front of the goal and another Forge player heads it into the net.

"Boom!" Jay stands to applaud, shaking her head and whistling again. The stadium erupts with boos from the locals while the small Pittsburgh fan section bursts into song.

I keep my eye on Wes, whose teammates crash around him for high fives after that assist. Is it my eyesight or does he wince when their center slaps him on the back? I've been noticing a lot of wincing from him lately…

The Forge dominate the play for most of the first half, spending the whole time up near the Charleston net, but they don't find another goal. Charleston kicks the ball out of bounds and for some reason, Wes moves to take the throw in. Jay notices this as well and asks, "Why the hell would they have a striker take the throw?"

Wes looks down the line to where his teammates are moving fast, sprinting to get open. He draws the ball back to throw it and it arcs over his head right to the foot of the charging Forge striker, who slams it into the back of the net, dead center. But I'm not looking at the celebration on the field. I'm staring at Wes, crumpled on the grass in pain.

CHAPTER 10
WES

WHEN I MANAGE to open my eyes, I see my uncle's face a few inches from mine on the sideline. "Is it your back, son?"

I groan in response, nodding a few times. The training staff makes their way over to me, patting me up and down like they're searching for blood. "Back," I grunt as another spasm rolls over me. Am I seriously hunched on my side in the grass a half hour into my first professional soccer game?

"Can you sit up, Wes?" The trainer, Randy, asks, offering a firm hand and tries to get me upright. I'm blowing air like a woman in labor as white-hot pain burns down the left side of my body. This is just like before when I was out for months with a bulging disc.

The same fucking injury, despite all my training, despite the care I've taken with my muscles. Hell, I even went to a flipping yoga class, and I'm still slumped against my trainer on the grass while an entire stadium whispers to themselves about whether I'm paralyzed.

Randy and Uncle Hawk get me to my feet, and I squeeze my eyes shut, dizzy with the pain. I hear the applause as I hobble to the bench, and I can just make out the announcer calling for a substitution. I've just fucked up the entire strategy Uncle Hawk had going into this match, but I guess I should find some comfort knowing we are at least up 2-0.

I realize they aren't steering me toward the bench at all but taking me down the hall to the training room. "Guys, at least dump me on the bench with the team. Come on."

"Come nothing," Hawk says. "You're worth more to me healthy and you're going to see the doctor."

I growl in response, eventually assuring him I can manage the walk with Randy in support. I know he has to get back out to the pitch. Before we can argue about it, Aunt Lucy appears at my side to help me the rest of the way to the table in the training room.

I collapse onto the table, eyes squeezed shut as the doctor pokes and prods, rubs me with Icy Hot, and hooks me up to electric stimulation for my aching muscles. The trainer quickly sticks a bunch of electrodes to my back and turns on the machine, sending waves of tingling sensation through my body. They drape a heating pad over my back and then, from the sound of things, someone else has blown their knee, so I'm left unattended to wallow in my misery.

"What happened?" I pry an eye open to find Cara Moreno staring into my face, her own etched with concern.

"Back. Probably a disc." I grunt in between pulses from the stim, feeling drowsy after the adrenaline disco my body just experienced. I feel her hand on my forearm, soothing me. I should probably respond in some way but can't get it together and I must start dreaming, because I think I hear my Aunt Lucy talking to Cara.

"Did you walk in here alone?"

"More like ran." Cara whispers, clearly upset. "I was worried about Wes."

"We had a plan in place, Cara. I told you he was going to be here. He's probably on his way into the training room right now for fuck's sake."

Cara's grip on my arm tightens. This must all actually be

happening. I hear her mutter an apology, asking if she can please stay with me until the MRI.

"MRI?" I lift my head at that, dislodging the heating pad on my back. Aunt Lucy shifts it back into place.

"Yeah, kid. Healthcare moves faster in the pros." She winks. "You're a hot commodity now. Did you know they're counting the throw-in as an assist?"

That draws a smile and a smaller, happier moan from me. I hear a flurry of voices in the room and Aunt Lucy says, "Well, I have to go. Cara, please stick with Wes, okay? And protest if they ask you to leave unless I come back for you."

The worried masses flock around the other guy with the knee pain and I hear a scrape as Cara drags a folding chair close to the table where I'm beached. "How long until they wheel me into the MRI? Did they say?"

"Dunno. It still blows my mind that Charleston has on-site imaging. You'd be on an ambulance right now if we were back home."

"Maybe I'll add an MRI machine to my contract demands when I renew."

I expect Cara to laugh at my joke. It feels so obvious to me that I'm probably going to be cut from the team once the scan reveals irreparable spinal damage. My parents' words echo through my head as the electrodes pulse into my damaged spine.

I open my eyes when I realize she's not laughing. She's just sitting with me, tracing her fingers up and down my arm like she doesn't know what else to do. Which is fine, because this feels nice. "You're so pretty," I blurt, turning my head to the side and pressing my cheek against the blue vinyl covering the table.

"Well, you're not half bad looking, Stag." Cara grins. I remember that I made huge assumptions and fucked up the opportunity we had to be together. It's entirely my fault she doesn't think I'm 100% good looking. But she's here. That has to mean something.

We're just on the cusp of being friends again … I don't even know if she wants more than that. It's probably just as well, since I doubt she wants to be seen with an unemployed former athlete with no college degree. Maybe I could join her fan club and keep making her lunch.

"Hey." I open my eyes again and her face is so close. If I could manage to lift my head up off the table, I could kiss her. I try it anyway, and my nose collides with her forehead as a ripple of sparks fires down my sciatic nerve.

"Fuck!" I slap the table in pain, more alert now that I've made an ass of myself and further irritated my back.

When I open my eyes again, Cara swallows. I watch the lovely line of her throat moving above the black polo shirt. The letters Hot Metal shimmer across her chest in red foil, a tiny Pittsburgh Women's Soccer embroidered in gold above one boob. "Would you like me to kiss you, Wes? Is that what you were trying to do?"

I snort. "Trying. Failing. Story of my life lately, I guess. Thought I could at least manage to kiss a woman, but nope." I pop the P, lulled into a drunken stupor again by the tens machine and the fumes of the menthol ointment on my back.

"How about this," she rests her hand on my cheek and smiles. Then she leans in and places the world's most chaste kiss to my forehead.

Before I can ask for more, the medical staff announces that it's time to stick me in the MRI tube.

CHAPTER 11
WES

THE PAIN MEDS make me drowsy, so I don't register that my family has filed into my apartment until I hear my mom wail. Her eyes brim with tears … unless that's the light playing tricks on me.

I'm sprawled on my stomach just aware enough to realize I drooled on my pillow. I'm pretty sure I'm naked. I know Uncle Hawk got me a first-class seat for the flight back so I could fully recline with heating pads, but that was peak muscle relaxer effectiveness, and I was super out of it. I guess my uncle got me into my apartment and dumped me into my bed too, but I doubt he'd take off my underwear.

Have I even showered since the game?

"Oh, Wesley." Mom runs a finger through my hair and climbs into the bed with me. "What happened?"

"Uh?" It feels like too much effort to turn my head, so I'm staring at the door when Dad leans through it before crossing his arms and frowning.

"Your aunt made you containers of food and your cousins are out in your kitchen making a chart for who is going to sit here with you, just until you're off the pain meds."

Mom tisks at him and pats my hand. "Thatcher, that's not necessary. I can be here the whole time."

"Emma, you cannot be here around the clock taking care of Wes *and* taking care of you. Remember your book launch?"

I notice Dad doesn't reference Mom's epilepsy, but I'm glad he's making her let my cousins pick up some of the work taking care of me.

Wait.

"I don't need people to take care of me." I find the will to roll onto my back, my arms following along on a few second delay from when my brain tells them to move.

"Is that so?" Dad walks over to my bed and squats on the floor next to it. I focus on the tattoos swirling around his forearms. I should get more tattoos. "When did you last take your meds? When are you due for another dose? When's your follow-up appointment with sports medicine here in Pittsburgh?"

"Thatcher, enough." Mom scolds him while rubbing my shoulder. I hope someone scrubbed me off so she's not getting sweat slime all over her hand, but I smell the menthol ointment on my pillow and know that I'm pretty scuzzy. "Wes, your cousins and I *want* to be here with you. Nobody will get in the way of your routines. We'll just hang out on your couch and use your Wi-Fi and make sure you take your pills."

Dad grunts. "And wipe your ass."

"I don't want anyone to wipe my ass. I definitely do not want my mother to wipe my ass."

Through narrowed eyes, I see my father squinting and rubbing his beard. "Do you think you can wipe your own ass right now?" He sniffs. "When's the last time you tried?"

"Thatch, you're being a lot right now." Uncle Hawk's voice of reason clears the fog in my brain, leaving room for frustration that my parents are bearing down on me like I'm still in preschool. "The team can send home health aides over twice a day until he's got more range of motion. I told the kids to set up a schedule to drive him to P.T., which will be the most important thing for his recovery."

"Health aides? Some untrained doofus earning minimum wage? I don't think so, baby brother. We've got this sorted." My dad's nostrils flare as he shakes his head.

My uncle starts arguing that the Forge pays good money for qualified professionals, and I tune them out as they bicker. I roll toward Mom, who has settled into the bed with her shoulders against my headboard. "Was Dad like this when you had seizures?"

She chuckles. "He used to bring me ham sandwiches. Oh, one time he sent a massage therapist to the house!"

I adjust my posture and wince in pain. "I'd take some of that right now. Better than him threatening to have Odin follow me into the bathroom."

"What if I just stayed over here for tonight? Would that be okay? You're still my baby, Wesley."

"I'm not going to kick you out of my guest room. But that's mostly because I can't stand up right now."

She plants a kiss on top of my head as the Stag family narrates their progress putting a care plan together. "Mom?"

"Yeah, kiddo?"

"Did Uncle Hawk say what the diagnosis was? From the MRI?"

She smiles a wobbly smile. "Herniated disc. Same as last time. Your father and I would like you to consider surgery."

I'm not in the mood to discuss this with my parents. I'm not going under the knife if I can continue to treat my spine with steroids and physical therapy. I know my parents don't want to hear me say I plan to get back on the field as soon as I'm able, so I just let the brain fog settle back in as I close my eyes amidst the din.

That's when I hear a female voice and realize I must be

dreaming. Cara laughs nervously and I hear her say, "I should have realized he'd have family here to support him. I'll come back another time."

Except maybe I'm not dreaming, because the mattress shifts as my mother climbs out of the bed. "Goodness, no, dear. How thoughtful of you to come see Wesley and ... did you bring him a cheeseburger?"

"Can he eat cheeseburgers?" Dad sniffs audibly, so I do, too. I smell Cara's meatloaf and pry my eyes open again.

"You're actually here?"

She nods and stands in the hall, shifting her weight from foot to foot. She's still dressed in her team polo and team sweats. She must have gone right home from the airport and made me a snack without even stopping to change first. My stomach swoops at the thought of her rushing to help me. I'm pretty sure my face splits into a dopey grin.

For once, the Stag family is silent as they stare at Cara, waiting for her to speak. I hope my entire family isn't out in the living room. It'd be better if just, say, six or seven of my cousins were looming over her at my door rather than the baker's dozen tall, lanky guys in peak concern mode.

Cara swallows and I try to sit up a bit. "I did bring a burger, but it's not actually a burger ... well, the patty is but the bun is mostly cheese and egg ..." She holds up the clear container and I grin, and for a minute I can't even feel my back hurting. "It's an illusion," Cara continues as my family just blinks at her until Dad clears his throat.

"Emma, why don't we all go down the street for a coffee and finalize the ride schedule like Hawk suggested. Wes can visit with his friend."

It feels strange to hear my father refer to Cara as a friend. The word seems totally inadequate, and yet more than I should be hoping for after how I treated her. We have such a tenuous companionship since I apologized, and I remember how she sat with me in the training room after my injury. It's got to mean something that she drove here with a special treat. Right?

I croak out the word "friend" groggily as Mom leaves my room. I hear murmuring and the sounds of footsteps in the hall, finally the thunk of my heavy door closing, and I sigh audibly. "It feels different when it's just us here," I tell her.

Cara sets the gift on my nightstand and bites her lip. "Nobody told me your prognosis. I've got your phone, though. Here." She sets something on the night stand next to the fake burger. "I gave your bag to Coach Lu—to your aunt."

"Herniated disc," I mumble. "My family will want surgery. I will opt for steroid injections and heavy P.T. If I'm not fired."

"Come on, Wes. They're not going to fire you over this. You had two assists in your professional debut."

"They've let good players go before."

"Your uncle isn't dumb. How long are you out?"

I stare at the ceiling. "Probably six weeks. So … you know … the rest of the season."

"Well, then you'll have the entire off season to really dig in. You'll be a beast by training camp."

I turn to look at her and her smile lights up her whole face. My brain tells my hand to reach out and stroke her hair or cup her cheek, but my arm doesn't listen to me and it just sort of flops around on the bed. Cara frowns at my chest and sniffs. "Have you showered?"

I shake my head. At least I think I do.

"Hm." I wonder if she's thinking of the last time we showered together. I definitely am, and the mental image would have me hard as hell if these pain killers weren't slowing all my reflexes. Or maybe I am hard? Cara leans closer. "I could help you. I think I could."

I love the idea of that, of her naked against me again,

soaping up my body while I watch the water bead off her nipples. God, I want that. But I know this isn't the time to make that leap. I want to do things right with Cara. I want to earn her trust back properly. I swallow. "My uncle said home health aides would come for that stuff."

"Oh." She seems disappointed, like I've rejected her. I can't trust anything I say right now.

"I want to watch you shower," I say, and she laughs. Maybe I'm doing okay here? "When I'm not on drugs I want you to help me shower. No. That's the wrong thing. Someday I want to shower you again, Cara. With your toes."

Cara laughs and I hear the door open again. My family must be back already. Cara rests a hand on my forearm and leans close. "I fly out to Germany in a few days with the national team. I came to tell you I'll be gone for two weeks …"

"I'll miss having lunch with you."

She laughs and nudges the fake burger so it's within arm's reach. "I expect you to watch the U.S. friendly matches on TV and discuss them with me when I get back."

"If the TV can find them, I'll only watch your butt." I hope I just told her I plan to watch every minute of her matches, even if she's on the bench. I might not have a career much longer. But I do have a woman I find fascinating. "Charge your phone?"

"I already packed my adapter." Cara winks. For a moment I think she's going to lean in and kiss me on the mouth, but my mom appears behind Cara.

"It is just so nice of you to think of Wesley. And to bring him a gift. I'm Emma Stag, his mother. I think I forgot to say that before."

"Cara Moreno." Her face blurs into my mother's red nest of curls in my drug-altered vision. "Wes, I'll see you when I get back, okay?"

I nod. At least this wasn't goodbye. I hope she doesn't realize I'm a limping has-been athlete already and ditch me for someone who can complete a throw-in without breaking his back. I fall asleep to the sound of my parents walking Cara out of my apartment.

CHAPTER 12
CARA

WES

Good luck today, Moreno. I'll be watching.

I'VE PROBABLY STARED at his text a thousand times since I woke up. It's funny. I was so convinced that a relationship would take my focus away from my game, get in the way of progress. The reality is that I'm somehow sharper knowing Wes is back home rooting for me.

It doesn't make sense. I've always had people rooting for me. Shante and Rosalie and Toni all plan to fly to Paris for the Olympics and have each convinced their local pubs to air today's friendly against Germany.

Not that it was a heavy lift. We play at 4pm, so that means Wes and Shante are watching me at ten in the morning their time. I find it hard to imagine Toni or Rosie will be awake and at a bar for soccer in their time zones.

I wonder if Wes will leave the house to watch the game or sit alone in his apartment, brooding. His injury rattled his family, and I can't help but wonder if that's what has him feeling so hopeless about the whole thing. I've seen athletes overcome much worse, and I know he can get back out there.

I'm lost in these thoughts in the hotel dining room, stirring muesli into my yogurt, when I hear shouting from the coaches' meeting in the conference room. Coach Akemi never loses her cool, but she's shrieking at someone with enough ire to freeze my arm in place.

"… change my coaching roster in the middle of an international tour?" The response is muffled, and Coach growls. "What happened to total autonomy to select my own staff? This is bullshit."

Coach bursts from the room and down the hall as my team stares after her. All of us had been pretty subdued pre-coffee, but Jay raises her brows at me from across the room. I shrug and then stiffen when I see Lou Rubeo exit the conference room. He looks around the dining room with a fake grin on his face and I slouch to hide myself behind the menu holder on the table.

By the time I straighten my spine, the rest of the Soccer USA staff is filing toward the elevator, silently, looking like we lost our match. I don't like feeling as if the opponent is the president of our organization, rather than the opposing team on the field.

I choke down a few bites of breakfast and decide to retreat to my room before our film session. I guess that's why I come across Coach Lucy in the hall, her tear-stained face red and splotchy as she stabs at the elevator button. "Oh, Cara." She sighs and smiles. "Good luck today. You don't need it, but I know you'll kick ass out there."

I frown. "You won't be there to see it?"

She shakes her head. "Unfortunately, no. But I don't want you to worry about that today, okay?" The elevator arrives and Lucy drops her bag in the door to hold it open. She pulls me in for a hug. "Stick with your teammates and play like you trained. I will be watching no matter where I am."

She backs into the elevator, picking up her bag, and the door slides shut, leaving me feeling confused and unsettled. I slip into my room and drink a glass of water. I check my phone again, stare at the message from Wes and realize he sent it in the middle of the night. I wonder if he was lying in bed when he did so.

That sends an entirely different set of sensations rioting through my belly, but it shakes me from my funk enough to head back downstairs. The team is gathered in the conference room ready for film, but Coach Akemi hasn't reappeared yet. I slide into a chair near the other midfielders. Sabrina, who plays opposite me, gestures for me to lean in. "They fired Lucy," she says, shaking her head.

"What?? When?"

Sabrina shrugs. "What I heard is Lucy filed some sort of complaint against someone on the office staff, and they responded by sending her home."

"In the middle of our tour? That's insane."

She's about to say something further when Coach Akemi walks into the room and sinks noisily into her seat at the head of the table. "You've all heard by now. We are without a fitness coach until the organization deems fit to provide us with a new one. My choice for this team was dismissed, but she left notes to get you all warmed up and then cooled down after today's match." She looks at a piece of paper in front of her on the table. "Prep swimsuits for after the game. Apparently, we're doing hydrotherapy."

She doesn't field questions, just reaches for the remote and turns on the video of yesterday's scrimmage, stopping every few seconds to zoom in on someone's positioning or compliment our passing. "We feeling good, folks? Ready to kick some German booty today?"

We all cheer a yes, but it lacks the energy we normally build when we're yelling en masse.

Our ride to the stadium is subdued. I can't tell if our warmup is as well or if this is just what it feels like to focus before a national team match. Jay finds me in the locker room and elbows me until I smile for a selfie with us in our jerseys. "This is for the mantle, Moreno. No, we should blow it up huge with a flag and a bald eagle canvas."

"You want me to take a pic of you guys?" Sabrina tugs at her navy shorts and Jay nods. We squeeze one another as we smile for Sabrina and, despite the situation with our coaching staff, the reality sets in. I'm wearing a USA national team jersey. I'm about to take the field for my country in a match against Germany. As long as I don't screw up out there, I will be back here in Europe for the Olympics in less than a year.

My smile is genuine and Jay air drops the picture to me. I send it to Wes, and he responds almost immediately.

WES

Red, white, and blue looks good on you two.

ME

That's my new favorite poem.

WES

Put the phone down and get out there already.

I do as he suggests. I think of him watching as I stand for the national anthem. I think of my friends back home and briefly wonder if my parents are tuned in. I quickly file those thoughts away with my questions about Coach Lucy as *too big for before the game*. And then I'm jumping in place, waiting for the ref to blow the whistle.

CHAPTER 13
WES

"ARE YOU UP, Wes? Oh, there you are."

"Shh." I wave a hand at my mom and raise the volume on the television. I don't need the announcer to tell me the German striker is pressuring Cara hard along the sideline, and I forget my mother is in the room when Cara manages to toe the ball back and fire a pass to her teammate. "Hell yeah! Get 'em." I try to rise and cheer, but then I remember that my back is still tender and the reason I'm home watching soccer on a Saturday morning is that I'm not with my own team in Phoenix *playing* soccer this weekend.

"What's this? USA?" Mom sits next to me on the couch and hands me a glass of juice. I see that she's got some pain meds in her other hand, and I frown, keeping my eyes on the television.

"Shh. Soon halftime."

Mom shakes her hand with the meds until I swallow them, and we both stare at the screen. I whoop when a German defender kicks the ball over the back line. "Yes! Corner."

I lean forward, ignoring the sting in my spine as the camera zooms in on Cara. I smile like a fool, watching her spin the ball as she waits for the ref. "Oh. Is that your friend? It is! The girl with the fake cheeseburger."

I ignore my mother as I watch Cara set up her kick. "Come on, come on." She nods her head and takes her shot. It soars up in front of the net and her teammate heads it in like it's nothing. "GOAL!" I stand, fists clenched, cheering, and I look over at my mom, whose face is stretched in a huge grin. The ref blows the whistle for half-time and I mutter a curse that the camera switches away from the on-field celebration. I was hoping to see Cara again, to stare at her beautiful face as she smiled after her assist.

"Anything you want to tell me, son?" Mom gestures at the television and hits mute on the remote as the commercials come fast and furious.

I sink back into the couch, heart racing. I loved watching my girl kick ass out there. And then I freeze, because I just thought of her as *mine* when she's anything but. Cara has so much going for her, so much to lose. She's said a bunch of times that she had to fight her entire family and centuries of the patriarchy just to slip that jersey over her head.

What have I got to offer her? Cases of beef jerky I'm not even supposed to lift for a few more weeks. I swallow. "She's my friend, Mom. We met at the camp in California."

"And now you both play here in Pittsburgh?"

I nod. She hums. "What?" I shouldn't snap at my mother, but I don't want to pull my eyes away from the screen.

"You know our family rules about safe sex, right, Wesley?" She rests a hand on my arm, and I whip my face toward hers quickly, which sends sparks of pain up and down my spine.

"Oh my god, Mom, yes. I know the rules. She comes first. She comes twice. Wrap it up. I know. Ow." I hear a rattling sound as Mom hands me a few pain pills, which I take from her without looking so I can watch Cara adjust her shorts before she takes a free kick. I followed all the rules with her, and I still blew my shot. But I'm working on it.

Mom taps at her chin and frowns. "Have you heard from your uncle today? I wasn't sure if Lucy called him since he's got to keep his head in his own game ..."

"I'm on injured reserve and Uncle Hawk is Coach Hawk right now."

"Mm. Well, you should know that Lucy got dismissed from the national team today. In fact, she's on a flight home right now." I turn my head to face my mother, slowly this time, eyes wide. She nods. "Your Uncle Tim is in stiff lawyer mode. It's quite impressive, as always."

I grab the remote from Mom as the game comes back on the screen for the second half. I don't want to blink for fear I'll miss a camera pan on Cara. This time, I focus on her face, trying to assess whether she's reeling from whatever went down with my Aunt Lucy. I wonder how the team will explain the optics of dismissing someone from their coaching staff mid-tour, when they still have two more friendlies to play before they head back to the states.

All I see is a woman focused on her game until Cara is subbed out at the 60-minute mark. I reach for my phone, sending her a quick message I know she won't see for hours.

> Terrific assist. Textbook corner.

And then I worry she will think I'm trying to mansplain her efforts, so I send a series of explanatory follow-up messages.

> Obviously I know you know that.

> I just mean it was great to watch. And I'm happy for you. You looked great out there.

"Wes, enough." I remember my mother is still here in my

apartment, eyeing me as I send rapid-fire texts to Cara. Mom grins. "You don't want to overwhelm her, bud."

I swallow and set the phone on the arm of the couch. I blow out a sigh. "You escorting me to PT later? Is that why you're over here today?"

She rubs my leg. "I'm over here because I love you, silly. But yes, it's my turn. I promise I won't try to stay and watch. I have to work on some edits anyway."

"Appreciate that, Mom." I glance at the screen. The US is still up 1-0 with a few minutes to go. I decide I wouldn't mind at all if Cara came with me to PT and watched me bear crawling across the gym and stretching out across the foam rollers. But she's got much bigger and more important things to do than sit around and stare at my recovery process.

I ask Mom about her book, hoping to shift the energy and distract me from my sorry state.

"I'm glad this one's about done." Mom frowns. "I might like to write another one about this situation with your Aunt Lucy. I don't like all the inequities I'm still seeing between the national teams. The men play at a much better time slot for an American audience, don't you think?"

I fudge my way through a conversation, not sure I want my investigative journalist mother delving into misogyny of American soccer when I'm just trying to claw my way back onto the payroll. But then I glance at the screen as the game ends, and I see Cara's face. She should be elated right now. She just claimed the assist for our nation's only goal in her first international match. But her smile is pinched, and her eyes seem hard.

"That sounds like an important book project, Mom."

She smiles and ruffles my hair. "I'm glad you think so, sweetie. You ready to start walking to the car?"

Slowly, with a lot of grumbling and questioning my life choices, I follow my mother to her Volvo.

CHAPTER 14
CARA

MY FIRST INTERNATIONAL tour with the national team isn't what I expected at all. I thought I'd feel a surge of pride exploding in my chest as I stood on the field while the national anthem played. I thought I'd wave at the camera and think of all the little girls watching, realizing they can do this someday.

Instead, it's been confusing and fraught. We won our games, but not like we should have done. The ghost of Coach Lucy's dismissal hovered around the bench, the locker room, the field itself. Nobody said as much, but I have to believe this was related to Lou Rubeo and what I confessed to Lucy about how he creeps me out.

I also think about Jay's comment that I am probably not the only woman he treats that way...if he felt bold enough to act like that where anyone could see, he probably worked up to that perceived invincibility gradually.

The long flight home is uncomfortable emotionally and physically, and when we land Jay mumbles that she's going to hire a rideshare back to our apartment rather than take the bus. I'm debating joining her as we head down the escalator to the baggage claim, but then I see a familiar face holding a sign.

Wes Stag stands leaning against a column, wearing a suit and a chauffeur's cap, holding a piece of cardboard with MORENO scribbled in black marker. The sight of him is so totally unexpected, and so welcome after all the travel, that I almost cry. Instead, a laugh bursts from my mouth. I jog down the final stairs to hug him and find myself surrounded by his familiar soapy scent as strongly as I'm circled by his arms. "What are you doing here? I thought you can't drive on your pain meds?"

He hooks a thumb over his shoulder toward a similar-looking man slouched on a bench, playing with his phone. "My cousin Wyatt is actually the driver." Wes shakes the sign. "Thought I'd make myself useful. Via my cousin."

I feel lighter than I did since Germany, when Lucy got sent away and Coach Akemi started shouting. Another laugh floats out of my parched throat and I hug him again, gently so I don't jostle his back. "This is such a nice surprise. Thank you." I glance at Jay, who has descended the escalator with a wide-eyed stare. "Do you have room in the car for one more?"

"I've got room for five more." Wes laughs. "We took our uncle's minivan since I didn't know how much stuff you had."

"More like you didn't trust me to drive your Jeep and I don't have a car."

"Anyway …" Wes waves at Jay. "We've got room for your goalkeeper. Jay, you want a ride home?"

She nods and jostles her way toward the clump of passengers waiting for bags.

"I'm Wyatt, by the way." Wes's cousin extends his hand. "I heard about you rolling by with fake burgers, but I was at a tournament in San Diego."

"Cara Moreno. And playing in Cali is marvelous in

autumn. Good for you!" A red light begins flashing above the baggage carousel and Wes moves like he's going to grab my luggage for me.

Wyatt claps a hand on his shoulder. "Not this time, cuz. Nothing heavier than a milk jug, remember?"

He sighs and shakes his head. "This fucking sucks."

I rub his arm. "I'm really sorry. You'll have to catch me up on what the PT said since I talked to you last. Was that when I was in Spain?"

"Look at you, playing so much international soccer you can't even remember where you've been." I suspect he's trying to avoid the subject, but I know I can get him to talk later. I'm surprised by how good it feels to anticipate talking to him alone.

Wes makes Wyatt pull Jay's and my bags as we wheel our way to an ancient minivan in short-term parking. "Shotgun," Jay shouts, and climbs up front, where she wedges her travel pillow against the window and falls immediately to sleep.

I smile at Wes in the captain's chair across the small aisle from me. "It's a little like that flight to Cali," he says, referring to the day we met, when the flight attendant was hitting on him during her safety spiel.

"Mmm." I yawn. "Except nobody in this vehicle is going to offer to blow your tube."

"That's going to be enough of that," Wyatt scolds from the front seat. He blasts heavy metal from the stereo and merges onto the highway, scowling. I know if I fall asleep now it will mess up my chances to get back on eastern time, so I force myself to stay awake on the ride home.

It helps that Jay knees the power button on the stereo and shuts off the music. She and Wyatt bicker about appropriate decibel levels until Wes suggests he turn this car around.

Jay flips both of them off. "Cara, don't get me wrong. I'm happy to save fifty bucks on this ride home. But your reindeer are driving me nuts."

"Reindeer?" Wyatt arches a brow and catches my eye in the rear-view mirror.

"That's what Jay calls the Stag family when she's feeling feisty."

"So, always, then," Wes deadpans, extracting bottles of water and granola bars from a pouch behind the driver's seat.

"Whose car is this again? These are delicious." Jay tears into her bar and I just nod in approval.

Wyatt explains, "My Uncle Ty retired from hockey to be a full-time dad." He shrugs. "All four of his kids are in college now, but he still stocks his dad wagon like he's hauling our entire crew to the playground."

The Bluetooth in the van picks up an incoming call on Wyatt's phone and we all listen to the robotic voice chant, "Incoming call from Unknown Number," before Wyatt growls and stabs the button to decline the call, which puts the heavy metal music back on until Jay growls and turns the music off entirely.

Jay guzzles her water and tosses all her trash into a tiny wastebasket in between the front seats. "I'm going back to sleep. Do not put that screaming music back on." She punches her pillow and closes her eyes again.

"So." Wes turns to face me, winces, and sets his spine in line again, facing forward while awkwardly trying to talk to me beside him. "You guys had a clean sweep."

I nod. "Yeah, Coach is pleased. We won't get a chance to train together for a few more weeks. And then we have a tournament in March …"

"And then Paris." Wes grins.

"So freaking cool, Cara." Wyatt drums his hands on the steering wheel as he waits to merge into the Fort Pitt Tunnel. I haven't lived here long enough for this view to get old, the way the city reveals itself in golden sparkles as we drive through the tunnel.

I press my face to the window as we drive over three

rivers in quick succession before the view fades into the highway embankments and overpasses. "Sorry. What was that?"

Wes is smiling again and shakes his head. "I was just saying you shouldn't let it go to your head, but I see you're still a Pittsburgh girl at heart."

"Our building is just up there." I point for Wyatt as he enters our apartment complex, and then I poke Jay in the shoulder to wake her up. "Thank you both so much for the ride home. Talk to you soon?"

I raise my brows at Wes, who furrows his and shakes his head. "I'll walk you up, if that's okay."

"Of course. It won't bother your back?"

"Nah. You've got an elevator, right?" Jay and I hoist our bags from the back of the van, and I notice Wes leaning through the window of the minivan. Wyatt waves and drives off. Wes slides his hands in his pockets. He's ditched the cap and jacket, loosened the tie, and has his shirt sleeves rolled up. The transformation has my heart racing. "Wyatt had an errand to run. He'll come back for me in a bit." He holds a hand up. "If I'm in the way I'll just wait for him outside. No pressure to host me."

"Don't be silly. Come on." I feel a strange second wind setting in and I think about the melatonin I bought in case I wanted help with the jet lag.

Jay slumps against the wall in the elevator, moving around with her eyes closed when we approach our floor. "I'm beat. I don't even have the energy to make jokes about you, Stag."

I pat her on the arm, still feeling alert myself. Probably because Wes is here... "Night, Jay." She waves and slams the door to her room, leaving her bag propped against the wall in the hall.

I chuckle and rest my own bag beside hers. We have a washer and dryer in the apartment and I'm sure our gear will be standing on its own by morning, but even if I'm too wired to sleep, I don't feel like doing laundry. "You want some water? I don't know if we have anything else."

"Water is great." Wes slowly lowers himself into the couch and I make my way over to him with two plastic Hot Metal souvenir cups of tap water. He holds his up to toast. "To Team USA."

"Salud." I smile as I drink. I feel at ease with him, like a piece of myself is missing when we're apart and I can be a whole person. Which is strange because I haven't known him long. I decide it's probably because we've already been intimate. Then I flush, remembering how he put my toes in his mouth ...

He clears his throat. "So, my family is in kind of an uproar. My aunt wasn't supposed to come home."

I set my cup on the table and let my head flop back on the couch. Wes angles his body toward mine, gingerly. "Wes, I just know it's about Lou Rubeo. I told her, you know ... how he made me uncomfortable and invaded my personal space."

"Cara, he touched you without permission. Not just a handshake type thing. That's harassment."

I close my eyes. "I know. And Lucy knows, and I'm sure she said something to someone ... and look where that got her."

"You know my uncle's law firm represents the interests of the Forge and the Hot Metal. Lucy won't take this lying down. She has an army of angry lawyers making a battle plan."

"Lawyers?" The word makes me shiver. Lawyers were always synonymous with austerity in my family. My parents got along just well enough to be civil to one another after they divorced, but not without footing extensive legal bills. I remember having to go to court, talking to judges about my living arrangements. It was terrible as a child. It feels even more daunting now, when all I want to do is play soccer.

"Yeah, Cara. Lawyers. Harassment is illegal. You have a right to feel safe at work." I swallow, unable to verbalize how those words impact me. I don't know if I feel unsafe per se. But I sure am distracted from my game whenever I know that man is anywhere nearby.

"I was just hoping Lucy would find some sort of solution where …"

"Where what? Someone would scold him, and he'd admit wrongdoing and knock it off?" Wes's eyes are wide with disbelief.

I sit up. "Yes. That is what I hoped would happen."

He scoffs. "Fat chance of that. If a guy like that has to be told not to treat colleagues that way, I don't think he's going to receive the message. Not really."

My body starts shivering. I'm not sure if it's the jet lag finally catching up to me or the weight of Wes's words. I reach for the water again, and my hand shakes so much the water sloshes onto my lap. "Here." Wes steadies my hand, guides it to my mouth so I can take a sip. "Are you okay? What can I do?"

I breathe in the scent of him. He smells faintly of menthol ointment. I've never seen him in dress clothes before and I take a moment to settle myself, staring at his forearm where it rests on my leg. I love the look of his dark arm hair over his pale skin, the green veins just visible beneath his powerful muscles. I lower my hand onto his. "I could really use a distraction right now, Wes…"

I lean toward him, ready for a kiss. I can see his chest rise and fall a few times before I close my eyes and then … nothing. He doesn't close the distance between us.

I open my eyes to see his boring into me, dark and sincere. He tips my chin up so our faces are level. I feel his breath whisper against my skin as he says, "You could never just be a distraction to me, Cara."

"Wes." My voice is a whisper. I don't know what to make

of this, of my attraction to him paired with his rejection of my physical advances.

He runs a finger through my hair and my body leans toward his touch. "You're exhausted and overwhelmed right now. When you kiss me again, I want it to be because you can't stand not kissing me." He swallows and I watch his throat work, remembering how it felt to lick along those cords of tendon. "We both have a lot going on right now. Huge, uphill battles to fight. I don't want to rush into anything physical and skip past the emotional stuff."

I breathe a few times, half in his arms, half arched away in rejection. I don't know what to say, how to tell him I feel a throbbing ache only he can calm … but also, he's probably right that I'm just looking to distract myself rather than really enjoy Wes Stag for all that he is.

"How about a hug?" His face is hopeful, and he twists slowly, gently to face me, opening his arms awkwardly.

I nod and sink against him, feeling him pull me tight, like I'm precious to him, like I'm the only thing that matters. Like I'm not some evil person who invites unwanted attention from Rubeo-type-men. Wes holds me and rubs my back and runs his fingers through my hair until I must fall asleep. When I wake up in the dark, I'm alone on the couch, but someone has tucked me under the comforter from my bed, a full glass of water beside me on the coffee table, my phone plugged in to charge beside my head.

CHAPTER 15
WES

I SWEAR, physical therapy at the sports medicine center is just as hard as training at the stadium. My therapist, Savage Sofiya, is a homicidal maniac, insisting I can lift more, stretch farther, and move faster than my body tells me. I show up every day, sometimes twice, and work until my muscles burn. I work until I barely think about Cara asking me to distract her and my dumb ass saying no. I know offering her a hug was the right thing to do, but that doesn't make me want her less.

Days out from holding her until she fell asleep, I'm drenched in sweat, chugging water, and fighting to concentrate as Sofiya growls at me to give her five more kilometers on the rowing machine, this time with resistance. "Are you serious? Haven't I been here for two hours already?"

"Is two hours too much for you? Should I call your coach?" Sofiya taps at her watch, and I growl, moping back to the sweaty machine with a sigh. By the time I'm done, I feel like an overcooked noodle, but I'm not allowed to stretch out and stick to the floor. Sofiya orders me over to the mats to stretch and cool down.

I comply, too tired to argue, until Sofiya blows a whistle and starts applauding. "Everyone! Wes just touched his toes! Look at that spine flexion!" The room bursts into applause and I realize I am indeed bent all the way over, fingertips on my sneakers.

"Huh." I hold the position a bit longer until I hear a familiar voice cheering louder than the others.

"You got this, Stag!" I look between my legs to see an upside-down Cara pumping her fist and cheering for me like I just scored a goal for the Forge. She puts two fingers in her mouth and whistles, and I didn't know she could do that. I straighten up, worried the sight of her will turn me on so fast I'll tent my shorts.

Sofiya pats my shoulder. "See you tomorrow, dude. Lots of water tonight."

"Yeah, yeah. Thank you," I add, backing toward the door and Cara, who grins and gives me two thumbs up. "You're here? I mean … I wasn't expecting you." I rake a hand through my sweaty hair. "I'm glad to see you."

"Glad to see me awake, you mean?" Cara laughs. "Wyatt reached out because I guess Jay left her headphones in the minivan. Yada, yada, I told him I'd bring you home today."

I grin, feeling my energy return at this news. Is it ridiculous that I'm excited she came to give me a ride home from physical therapy? I should be embarrassed by how excited everyone here is that I touched my freaking toes. But considering a few days ago it hurt to twist sidewise in a conversation, I guess I should let myself feel proud of this milestone.

"You ready?" Cara twirls her keys around one finger. "Although, if you're rowing and touching toes now, does this mean you can drive again?"

I shrug and refill my water bottle at the fountain, reaching for my phone and house keys from the little cubby where I stash my stuff during PT. "I stopped taking the narcotic pain relievers days ago, so probably. I see the doc again tomorrow afternoon." Cara falls in step beside me on the walk through the massive building. There are full-size athletic fields inside and most of the professional sports teams in Pittsburgh use the facility for medical support.

I'm overcome with an urge to wrap my arm around Cara, pull her close against my side as we walk. I resist it, though, because I don't want to send her mixed messages after I turned her down for a kiss in her apartment the other night. But I also don't want to just climb in her car and have her drop me off right away. I squint into the bright sky as we push open the doors to the parking lot. The facility is located along the river, and a bike path meanders by. I scratch the back of my neck and ask, "do you want to go for a walk or something? Are you free?"

She smiles and nods. "Sounds nice."

I gesture toward the trail as a cyclist breezes past. "You know, this goes all the way to D.C."

Her brows lift. "Seriously? How far is that?"

I shrug. "Dunno. Maybe a few hundred miles? I think my Uncle Ty and Aunt Juniper rode their bikes on it once, though. Took a few days."

"I bet that's gorgeous this time of year."

All around us, the trees are bright yellow, dropping oblong leaves that crunch under our sneakers. It is beautiful, but not like her. "You're gorgeous," I blurt, regretting my lack of filter. "I mean—"

She touches my arm. "Thank you, Wes. You're not bad looking. Especially all bent over to touch your hairy toes."

I nudge her with my shoulder, enjoying the fact that it doesn't hurt for me to do so. "Hey, about the other night … I just wanted to tell you, I'm not *opposed* to kissing you. You know that, right?"

Her cheeks flush, and I like that look even more than the sight of her here among the yellow leaves. "I guess I know that." She runs her hands through her ponytail and looks at me sideways. "It'd be easier if we just banged it out and ignored all the other stuff, though."

"Ha. Maybe." I rub my back. "Hey, can we sit? I don't want to overdo it."

"Of course!" Cara rushes to the side of the trail and brushes dried leaves and twigs from a bench overlooking the rusty old steel mills. "You all right?"

I nod. "Yeah. Just got tired all of a sudden." I stretch an arm along the back of the bench, and she leans into it. We watch a barge chug up the river. "Do you want to talk about any of the stuff with the national team? Have you seen Aunt Lucy since you got back?"

Cara sighs and slouches against the bench. "I really don't like talking about it. But I will if you want to." She presses her lips together. "Practice with the Hot Metal has been fine the past few days. But I haven't talked to Lucy alone, no. Maybe I'm avoiding her?"

I let the hand stretched along the bench rest on her shoulder and give her a squeeze. "It's all just so gross. I hate when people make other people feel small. Or powerless. I feel really powerless right now with this stupid injury and that's not anything near the same scale as what you're dealing with."

"What do you mean? You can't even play right now."

"Yeah, but I'm not ever—for any amount of time—worried someone sees me as anything other than an athlete." My eyes bore into her, and I think again of Lou Rubeo touching her, thinking he has the right to her body. If he walked by in this moment, I worry I'd strangle him. To me, Cara is power and grit personified, and I got the biggest rush of my life when she invited me to touch her, when she chose to be intimate with me. Knowing some man is out there trying to take that choice from her fills me with blinding rage. I stuff that back down, though, because she doesn't need my ranting and raving.

We sit in silence for a few minutes and then head back to her car. She cranks up some pop music and drums on the steering wheel as she heads west. "Oh, hey." She glances over at me, and my breath catches again at the sight of her golden skin in the sunlight, brown eyes smiling brightly. "Are you up for yoga again this weekend? We have a bye …"

"I'd love that. Man, what have I become? A guy who likes yoga."

"It's good for us."

"Yeah, yeah. But yes—maybe I can even drive us."

CHAPTER 16
WES

IT TURNS out I am indeed cleared to drive, and I celebrate this independence by hauling my carcass to PT for early sessions so I can still watch film and sit in on strategy talks with the Forge.

My uncle acknowledges my presence in the room with a tip of his chin and continues explaining a new formation he wants to try in our playoff match against Detroit. Unless this turns out to be a miracle strategy, this will probably be the last game of the season. I'm actually glad I made plans to go to yoga with Cara during it, because I need the distraction from all the emotions it brings up knowing my first pro season was such a glorious disaster.

"We'll miss you out there, buddy." One of the other strikers, Alejo, holds a hand out for a shake.

I give him a small smile in return. "Wish I could be with you guys. Man, it was brutal watching that game against Richmond. You were a beast."

Alejo pretends to brush dirt off his shoulder and we both laugh. "I'll see you around."

I spend the rest of my night wondering if it's too pushy for me to call Cara. I'm utterly distracted, wishing I could be with her for all my meals, wanting to text her during all the long pauses where I don't have any other human interaction. Maybe it was a mistake to live alone … especially when I'm so used to my family surrounding me at all hours.

Or maybe I'm totally smitten by Cara Moreno and letting it get in the way of my mental recovery work.

Whichever it is, I'm super early to pick her up in the morning and my mood immediately lightens when she climbs in my car smelling like clean cotton, wearing bright blue leggings and a fitted workout tank that hugs her taut abdomen.

I spend the entire drive to the studio wondering why exactly I turned her down for hot sex, especially knowing how explosive we are together.

"This might be the last time we get to hang out for a bit." Cara talks around a hair tie between her teeth as she works all her dark waves into a ponytail.

"I'll bite. Why's that?" The Hot Metal are also in playoffs, but I don't get the sense anyone expects them to advance much into October. The Forge are about to wrap up. I sort of thought we'd both have even more time on our hands.

"I overheard Lucy and your coach talking about you."

"You were eavesdropping?" I tease her, but I love that she was nosing around, interested in me. I love that I'm in her thoughts like she invaded mine all last night.

Cara pats her hair and smiles. "I think the medical team might clear you for off-season training."

"Ah, but that assumes the off-season starts tomorrow. Are you saying you don't have faith in the Forge today?"

"Without you? Not a chance."

I spend the entire rest of the drive glowing from her praise, but trying to be cool so Cara doesn't see how much her words affect me.

We bend and stretch our way through the class side by side, and my back doesn't bother me once. It's stunning how a few weeks of powerful muscle relaxants and intense physical therapy have me almost back to fighting shape.

It's even more incredible that we're in a room with what appears to be half the professional hockey team, and Cara hasn't even sent a lingering glance toward any of the beefy men surrounding her in Yoga for Athletes. I know because I've spent all my calming breaths watching her. She is, of course, focused on her breathing, and keeps her eyes on her own toes.

Cara has short-term goals she needs to achieve, an arc she has to complete this year with the national team. I remind myself that I'm a diversion for her. She said as much the other night. I blow out a breath, glad I said we should take things slow. Both of us have a lot on the line.

At the end of class, Cara seems totally blissed out in corpse pose and I feel like I have ants in my shorts, so I duck out of the room early to get a drink and wait for her where I won't disturb anyone. I check my phone and sure enough, I have a voicemail from the Forge team doctor.

"Wesley, Dr. Dansey, Forge Football Association. I reviewed your case with your physical therapist, read your files, and looked over your most recent images. I'm happy to clear you to return to off-season workouts with the team starting in two weeks, barring any spectacular on-field episodes today. Any questions, you know how to reach me."

I like how he ends the call without a sign-off. I aspire for that level of efficiency someday, like my Uncle Tim. Just brusquely offering the most important bits of information and saving any other niceties for his family.

And Cara. I'd be nice to her regardless of anything else happening in my life. The thought warms me, and I finally see her emerge from the studio, smiling and walking slowly, like she's drunk on endorphins.

"Hey." She drags out the vowel sound, gliding toward me

in her bare feet as I fish both of our sandals from the cubby we shared when we arrived.

"You were right about your gossip." I show her the phone screen with the automated transcript of the voicemail. "I'm back to work."

I can't rein in the grin that splits my face, but I almost fall over when Cara squeals and places her hands on my shoulders, stretching up to kiss my cheek. I feel the warm echo of her lips on my skin as she dances and claps. "Wes! That's fantastic. I'm so happy for you."

I rest a palm to the place where she kissed me, smiling so hard I wonder if my face will crack. "Can I take you out? To celebrate?"

Cara turns her head, brow arched mischievously. "You mean like a date? Because I have to tell you, Wesley Stag, I'm going to expect a goodnight kiss at the end of a date."

I lean against the wall with one arm raised, my best grin flashing all my teeth at her. "Oh, it's absolutely a date, Cara."

CHAPTER 17
CARA

"JAY, how are her feet looking? Don't lie to us." Shante shouts from the video chat in my bathroom as I get ready for my date. By which I mean styling my hair and trying to locate some makeup that isn't crusty or expired.

Jay pokes her head in the door. "She's wearing socks, chicas. But I'm guessing they're pretty rough."

"He's not going to see my feet." I shout this around a mouth full of hair pins as I try to tame my mop into an up do. I give up and decide to comb it instead, since I never wear it down and it's looking nice and shiny today.

"We just want you to be ready, querida." Rosalie waggles her eyebrows. "It's been a minute for you, right?"

I glare into the camera and my friends laugh. "Do I criticize your grooming choices from afar? No. I do not. Shante, were your feet supple and smooth when you went out with that person from the finance department?"

Toni cackles.

Shante wags a finger at me. "My feet were perfect, as always." She rocks back in her chair and wiggles her toes at the camera. "I'm telling you, since I stopped playing footy, I can play footsie instead. My finance sweetie approves."

I frown at her as I yank a comb through my hair one final time. "They saw your toes on your first date?"

Toni clears her throat. "This isn't exactly your first date with Wes, though."

Jay, who apparently stayed in the bathroom for the conversation, grunts. "Those two hang out all the time. And I like it because it involves free food for me, and sometimes rides from the airport." I stare at her. She shrugs. "He seems really into you, Cara."

Toni, Rosalie, and Shante collectively sigh so hard I think heart emojis might shoot out of my phone.

I bite my lip. "I don't know if I'm ready for *really into me,* though. I'm dealing with…" I flip my hands around in the air in what I hope is an all-encompassing gesture. "And, you know, I'm training for the Olympics."

"Yeah you are, chica!" Toni blows me a kiss and I smile.

"Look, I don't want anyone to suck on my toes today. But I wouldn't mind a little tonsil hockey."

"Gross." Jay throws a clementine peel at me. "Please don't call it that."

There's a knock at the door and my friends unleash a series of giggles and whoops. "I'm hanging up. I still have to finish in here." I end the call before they can protest, hurrying to swipe gray shadow on my eyelids. "Can you let him in and tell him I'll be out in a minute?"

Jay rolls her eyes and heads toward the front door. I hear her whistle, followed by muffled voices as I dab mascara on my lashes, and I finally locate a tube of lip gloss that seems like it's in good shape. Some of my teammates wear a full face of makeup if they know a match is going to be televised. Me? I have to beg and borrow supplies when my name gets called for a press conference. But I want to feel special tonight, so I take some extra time emphasizing my features. I step back from the mirror and smooth my hands down my dark jeans.

I found a loose-fitting hunter green sweater that hangs off

one shoulder and I managed to cram my bulging pro-soccer calves into a pair of brown leather boots that stop just below the knee. I have no idea where Wes is taking me on short notice, but I figure this outfit will work unless it's someplace really fancy. I hope it's not someplace swanky.

I step into the hall and Wes stops his conversation with Jay at the sound of my shoes on the floor. I smile, watching his eyes widen at the sight of me. He looks pretty damn good himself in a ribbed turtleneck and black jeans. "Hey." He grins but his eyes dart over to Jay and he hesitates. "You ready to head out?"

"Be safe, you two." Jay laughs at her own joke as she grabs her keys and a puffy vest. "I'm going to a movie with the strikers. I'll be late on purpose." She winks and leaves as I shift my weight.

Wes walks toward me, and he smells delicious. I sense a subtle cologne or maybe aftershave. "Cara, you're gorgeous." He reaches out a hand to touch me, like he can't help himself, and I lean my head into his palm.

"Thank you. You look nice, too."

He tips his head toward the door. "Come on. I have a surprise for you."

"Shouldn't I be surprising you?" I lock up and follow him down the hall toward the stairs. "You're the one with the big news this week."

Wes drapes an arm around my shoulder as we walk toward his car. "Just let me show you the surprise."

We drive a few blocks, over a bridge, and head up toward Wes's neighborhood. The Allegheny river is beautiful in the dark, with all the city lights reflecting off the water. Wes parks outside a brick building that looks like it once housed a factory of some kind.

He rushes out of the car to open my door and extends a hand toward me as I climb out of the car. "Okay, so, this place isn't open yet."

"Then why are we here?" I frown, looking at a few windows where light shines from inside.

Wes shakes his head. "I mean it's not open to the public. My aunt—the chef—hooked me up with the owner when I said I needed to find a place I could take you that would fit with your meal plan for the national team."

"Wes, that sounds like a lot of hassle. I thought we'd be—"

He holds up a hand as we approach the door. "Turns out the owner of this place is a huge football fan. Moved here from Spain. She couldn't wait to bring us in to test things out with her staff and her menu and whatnot."

Wes tugs the door open to reveal a space under construction. I can see exposed brick walls and shining floors, but he guides me toward a set of stairs. We make our way up a few flights, and he pushes open a door to the rooftop. I gasp at the beautiful, intimate space.

Cushioned benches are arranged to look over the river, with a low table set with candles. There's room up here for a few tables, but it seems tonight it's just us up here. Strings of fairy lights ring the balcony, and a fire crackles in a low grate.

Wes lifts my hand and kisses my knuckles, his lips warm against my cool skin. "Do you like it?"

"I love it." My voice is a whisper and I let him guide me toward the bench, where he snuggles up close to me. The fire warms us from behind and I look around, enjoying the muffled sounds of the cars on the roads below. It all feels so far away while Wes is so close, like the two of us are nestled in a secret perch.

I hear the door open and turn my head to see a server dressed in black, carrying a tray. "Good evening, Ms. Moreno, Mr Stag. Chef sends some water infused with rosemary and ginger for you to enjoy while you look over tonight's menu."

He hands me a dainty glass with a sprig of herbs garnishing the cool liquid. The menu is hand written on card stock and I gasp again when I see the list of courses. Everything from the almond crusted zucchini appetizer to the tarragon chicken to the yuzu tart dessert fits easily into my food parameters. But unlike the bland chicken and veggies Jay and I subsist on most of the time, this meal promises to burst with flavor and texture.

"Wes. This is incredible." I take a big gulp of my water, overcome with excitement for a restaurant meal I'm actually able to enjoy.

"You're pretty incredible, Cara. I'm not just saying that."

My cheeks heat and not from the fire.

The server returns with the appetizer and asks if we're interested in anything else to drink. I bite my lip. "I'd love a glass of red wine with the main course if you could recommend something?"

He smiles and nods. "Yes, indeed. I recommend the tempranillo with tonight's flavor profile. For you, sir?"

"I'll have the same, please. And maybe a pitcher of this water in the meantime?"

Wes offers me the plate of nutty zucchini discs, and I pinch one with my fingers, seeing no silverware yet. "Oh god, this is amazing." We both chew and moan about the delicious veggies until the plate is clear.

At some point, our server comes to clear the appetizer and delivers soup and salad so quietly I barely notice. Wes adjusts his posture, I assume to accommodate his sore back, and I miss the closeness of his body even if it's easier to eat as we're seated more upright.

"I wanted to really go big this first date since I'm not going to see much of you for a bit." Wes winks as he spears asparagus wrapped in cured meat.

"Well, I'd say you hit the back of the net. Mmm." I snag the final roasted pepper from our salad plate and take a quick bite. "But not gonna lie, I'm really excited for Palo Alto. If we beat Jamaica we'll be in amazing shape for the group stage."

He listens while I rattle on about each country's prospects

at the Olympics, and at some point, he starts rubbing my hand with his thumb as I talk. It feels so natural, this physical connection but also spending time with him in this romantic setting. I don't have a flutter of nerves, perhaps because we've already seen each other naked.

But I did expect at least a little unease. Instead, I just bask in the glow of him, his warm smile, this entire thoughtful experience.

He clears his throat and rests his hand flat on top of mine, asking, "Who did Coach Akemi name to replace Aunt Lucy?"

And there's the ball of lead hitting me in the stomach. "Not sure who it is. Some guy from Texas, I think? He emails all the workout plans and such. We'll meet him at the camp."

"Surprises me that she picked a dude. Isn't everyone else on the staff female?"

I smile. "Yeah, Coach Akemi is big on women leading women. Well…" I think about Coach Bev, from the men's team. "I guess she's just big on women in leadership positions."

Wes grunts. "Would be great if she had more sway in the national team office."

I groan. "I wonder if we win a gold medal if that will give her more pull? Akemi was so, so angry when they fired Lucy without her input."

Wes sits back in his chair and looks at me intently, considering. "Have you told anyone about what happened? Other than my aunt?"

I shake my head. "I keep hoping that was the end of things, that he knows she knows and will maybe watch his step or something." I adjust my posture and drink some water. "We have a new rule that Coach Akemi kept up even after Lucy left—we always travel with a buddy in the stadium. It's been good for a lot of reasons, actually. The press sometimes sneaks in and tries to catch players off-guard with questions we're not supposed to answer."

"They do that sometimes with us, too." Wes's eyes shift toward the door, and I smell the savory warmth of our main course.

Our server sets down our chicken and a glass of wine for each of us. "Buen provecho," he says with a bow.

"Gracias por todo," I respond and the server winks at me before backing down the stairs, leaving us alone with our drinks and our meal.

"It's pretty hot that you speak another language." Wes nods his head in approval. "Americans really suck at that kind of thing."

"I am American." I nudge him with my boot, and he concedes my point with a wince.

"Sorry. I just did that thing where I forget that we don't have a national language or universal heritage."

"Mmm hmm." I grin at him. "Te salva que eres bello."

He lifts my hand and kisses my knuckles again. "What does that mean?"

I wink. "I basically said it's a good thing you're hot."

"I'll take it."

CHAPTER 18
CARA

WES RAISES his glass and I clink mine against him, savoring the taste of the wine. One glass should be fine with my meal plan, especially considering everything else here is on the list of "knock yourself out" foods.

I don't want this date to end. Between the food and the spicy wine and the ambiance, it feels like some sort of fairytale. Plus, Wes has been staring at me intently for hours now and I could melt under the heat of his gaze.

"I want to do better with you, Cara. I want to be a better friend and listen more, and I want to be here cheering for you as you crush it with the national team."

The smile splitting my face might strain my face muscles if I'm not careful. "You are a good friend, Wes. Thank you." I rub at his leg with my foot, gently this time, and his promise of a goodnight kiss starts to feel really inadequate for what I'd like to do with him right now.

Wes scoots back around the bench so he's sitting right next to me again, our cleaned plates off to the side. I remember that we haven't yet had dessert, and just as Wes slides an arm around my shoulder, our server reappears with a tart and two spoons. "Here you are, sir, madam. And you can take all the time that you need." He ducks away before I can thank him, and I turn my head back to Wes to see him aiming a spoonful of yellow custard at my mouth.

He tilts a head in question, and I open my lips. Wes slides the quivering spoon of tangy citrus into my mouth, and I nearly die of bliss right there on the rooftop. "I've heard you make those sounds before," he whispers.

I'm sure my pupils have dilated fully by now. "Doesn't even compare. You have to try this." He opens his mouth like a baby bird, and I swat at his chest, but I don't want to deprive him of this delicacy, so I spoon some custard up for Wes and feed it to him, gently.

"Oh shit." His face brightens as he works through the seven stages of ecstasy involved in this dessert. I balance the plate on his long thigh and the two of us press close together, sharing an orgasmic flavor experience that's heightened by my desire for him. Based on the size of his pupils and the ragged breaths he draws whenever I press on his leg for leverage as I scoop up yuzu, Wes feels the same level of barely contained lust.

"Take me home." I place the spoon back on the empty plate with a clang. Wes nods and springs to his feet, tugging my hand and guiding me down the door.

The white-clad woman at the foot of the stairs must be his aunt's friend, the chef who created our feast. She speaks with a heavy accent as she asks us how we enjoyed our meal. I beam at her. "Muchas gracias. La cena estuvo deliciosa."

Wes, standing behind me, pinches my butt and I jump. "What she said. Gracias. Truly."

Chef winks at me and I yelp as Wes hauls me out to the car.

His hand splays across my thigh as he drives back to my apartment, and I feel the heat radiating from his body as we finally climb the steps to my door. When Wes finally presses my back against the door and leans his body against mine, my knees threaten to buckle. "Cara, I can't get you out of my head." His voice is ragged, almost pained.

"I don't want you to," I whisper. And it's true. Above all the stress and the intensity of work, I have Wes Stag as a comforting, sexy blanket. He makes me laugh. He takes me for fancy food. And he'd better kiss me, or I will actually burst.

His face hovers an inch from mine until he grabs my face with both hands, pulling my mouth against his.

I moan, sliding my tongue into his mouth, the taste of him familiar and fascinating. Deep sounds of pleasure rumble from Wesley's chest and his hands move to my back, my butt. I rock my hips against his as he nibbles my lower lip, feeling the thick bulge inside his pants and loving that I put it there.

I let my head tilt back against the door as Wes sucks on my neck and licks his way from my throat back up to my mouth. "I want you." My voice is so assertive when I meant for it to sound sexy. And maybe it does, because he growls and pulls his head back so he can meet my eye.

"Are you desperate for me, Cara?" I nod and he thrusts his hips against mine, pushing me back against the door with delicious pressure. He grazes a knuckle down my chest, not quite touching my nipple through the layers of sweater and my bra. I whimper at the tease. "I could make you come on my hand right here in the hall. Would you like that?"

Another nod and I lunge my mouth toward his, our teeth knocking together with the force of my kiss. I groan as Wes's long fingers crawl along the hem of my sweater, finding their way inside and into the waist of my jeans. "Yes," I breathe, letting my own hands trail along his chest. His body is firm and his heart thunders beneath my palms. I tilt my hips as his finger makes its way inside my panties.

"Oh, fuck, Cara, you do want this, don't you?" I whimper as he traces the needy bundle of nerves, not yet applying the pressure he knows I need.

"Let's go inside." I reach behind me for the door, fumbling for the knob, forgetting that I have the keys in my clutch that I seem to have dropped on the floor.

Wes rests his forehead against mine and presses harder against my clit. I forget what I was just asking him, what I needed. Nothing exists apart from that exploring digit and the heat of him holding me up. "Let me see, Cara. Come for me. Show me."

My mouth falls open, but no sound emerges. We stare into each other's eyes and my hands freeze with his shirt bunched in my fists. Wes circles and presses, his long fingers sliding along my seam as his thumb presses firmly against my clit. "So wet," he whispers. "So slippery for me."

I nod my head and feel a burst of energy erupt behind my belly button. The ball of pleasure rolls toward my center, throbbing and pulsing until it ripples through my entire body. Gasping and rocking, moaning and shivering, I come on Wes Stag's hand just like he asked.

He cups my sex until the waves subside and then slides his hand from my jeans as my breathing slows. I stare at him through half-closed eyes as Wes lifts the finger that had just been inside me, to his kiss-swollen lips. He sucks his finger, and my hands drop to my sides as he growls. "Delicious."

"Wes."

"I love hearing you say my name. Have I told you that before?" I shake my head. "Well, I love it." He bends toward me, kissing me gently. I see and feel his bulge inside his jeans, and I extend a hand to reach for his length. Wes steps back.

"Wes?"

He kisses my forehead. "I still want to go slow. Is that okay?"

"That was slow for you?" My eyes fly open finally as I start to take in that we are not going to have penetrative sex.

"No, Cara. That was slow for *you*." He kisses me gently and swallows, smiling. His hands are on the door on either side of my head, and I can smell my arousal still clinging to his fingers.

"What about you?" I glance down at his crotch, seeing his junk twitch beneath his jeans.

"I will dream of the sight and sound and taste of you coming for me, Cara, the whole time you're gone."

A thought occurs to me, and I bark out a laugh. "Are you saving the milk until I buy the cow? Is that how the saying goes?"

Wes cocks his head to the side, a crooked grin lighting up his face. "I just want to give you something to look forward to when you get back." I swat at him again. He grabs my hand and kisses it, palm-side up this time, with a naughty lick. "But seriously, Cara, we both have so much on the line. I don't want either of us to be distracted from our work right now."

"You're not a distraction, though. You're …"

"You told me you need a distraction."

I shake my head. "I thought you'd get in my head and strain my focus, but it's the opposite, Wes. You keep my mind off the bullshit."

"Cara, you need to sit with the bullshit. You need to work through it until it doesn't have any power over you. I don't want to be a distraction from the bad stuff. I want to be…" Wes drags a hand through his hair and shakes his head. "I want to be the man who makes you feel seen and understood and celebrated."

His words hit me like a kick to the shins, knocking my breath away with their impact. A hot tear rolls down my cheek and Wes brushes it aside with his thumb. He stoops to pick up the bag I dropped and reaches in it to hand me my key ring. With the echo of his words still ringing in the air, he presses one final kiss to my lips and smiles, not as brightly as before. Wes waves and walks down the hall.

CHAPTER 19
WES

IT'S BEEN a week since Cara left for California and I swear I can still taste her, still smell her hair. Memories of our date keep me up at night, in a good way, and the anticipation of a repeat keeps me focused during off-season training sessions.

Uncle Hawk keeps saying he's only looking for 80% effort during our scrimmages and drills, but I feel like I'm pouring out 110% just to keep up with the guys at their relaxed pace. I'll get there, though.

As I drive to the stadium, my bluetooth tells me I have an incoming message from Cara. "Shall I read it aloud?" I get a kick out of the British accent I set for the robot voice in the car, and I talk back to her like she's a real person.

"Please do, darling."

She responds in her slow, monotone. "Cara Moreno says game tonight against Jamaica wish you were here they moved me to false nine."

"Oh shit!" Cara had been hinting that her coach was playing around with some different formations. Cara usually plays deep midfield, like Uncle Hawk did, which is pretty grueling since she's involved on defense and offense. False nine puts her up closer to the opponent's goal.

"Darling, please respond to Cara Moreno."

"Sure, Wesley. I can do that. What would you like to say?"

"Holy shit exclamation point that's incredible period I can't wait to watch period."

My British robot repeats the message to me, and I tell her to send it, noting that it's pretty early in the morning on the West Coast. I'll have to check the game schedule and make sure I get the time difference right. We just have a short cardio workout this morning, so it shouldn't be a problem.

I stroll into the locker room, nodding at the guys. Most of the team are wearing headphones and scrubbing the sleep from their eyes. Our nutrition guidelines are a lot looser in the off-season and I'm pretty sure I can smell the alcohol wafting off our starting goalie. I haven't made much of an effort to hang with the team. It felt weird since I was injured and unable to play for the end of the season. I've just been chilling with my cousins in their apartment, playing video games like we've always done.

"Wes!" My uncle sticks his head out of his office and beckons me over. I yank my practice jersey over my head and click over to him in my cleats.

"Yep?"

"Can I get a ride with you to family dinner? Lucy drove this morning and she's … not feeling sociable today."

"Sure." I had forgotten about family dinner, which is dumb because it's been going on every Sunday since before I was born. I guess what I really did was forget today is Sunday. "I might have to leave early, though."

"Hot date?" Uncle Hawk waggles his eyebrows.

I sniff. "No. I'm watching the US versus Jamaica game." I hesitate before adding, "Cara's starting."

He purses his lips, and his brows lift in a "well, well, well" sort of expression. "Gotcha. Well, that match is the reason for my wife's foul mood today. I'll watch with you, if that's okay? Avoid the bear and all that."

I want to ask him more about Lucy's response to her dismissal from the national team, but I also want to get my mind ready for training this morning. I tell my uncle he's welcome to a ride and I head out to the field to warm up.

I think about Cara trying a new position as we run agility ladders. I imagine how her brain must be in overdrive, learning new places she has to be on the field, new patterns of running. I decide to shake things up myself, leading with my left foot when I'd normally use my right, and so on. It works great and I find I'm faster than I expected at this stage of my recovery.

I test out a longer stride on some sprint drills, too, and it feels weird but puts me over the line ahead of the other strikers. I was so worried that starting any sort of meaningful relationship with a woman would take me out of my game. I feel giddy as I realize that just thinking about Cara inspires me to go deeper into my training.

My face hurts from smiling in the last set of wind sprints and when my uncle blows the final whistle, he calls everyone in to a huddle. "Men. Can we all give a 'hell yeah' to Wes for that performance today?" The guys pat me on the back. "Inspirational recovery, kid. Hell yeah on three."

―――――

By the time I finish showering and changing into clean sweats, Uncle Hawk is waiting for me on a bench in the locker room. He holds up his phone. "Good news. Your Uncle Ty is going to put the game on his giant television, and we'll all watch together."

I open my mouth to protest that I won't be able to focus with a thousand Stags gabbing and cracking jokes, but Uncle Hawk holds up a hand. "Everyone knows we're there to support Cara and the rest of the national team. Your mom is still gunning for you to bring her around to meet the family properly some time, by the way."

I grunt, remembering my mother not-so-subtly bringing up my sex life the last time we hung out. "Mom is a sucker for anyone who makes care packages."

We drive to my aunt and uncle's house and I can tell we're among the last to arrive. The entire block is lined with SUVs, which are probably an impractical choice for city living, but most other cars are too small to accommodate the long-legged Stag men.

Chaos erupts from within as we open the front door, and I smell onions and tomatoes simmering in the kitchen. "We're going to eat chili while we watch." Uncle Ty bellows from behind a stack of bowls he starts lining up on the kitchen island, which is tricked out with every topping anyone ever thought might go with a vat of chili. But because this is Pittsburgh, there's also a bucket of French fries.

I notice that my family has saved me a coveted spot on the couch to watch the game. My cousins are all sprawled out on the floor and my aunts are chatting with Mom at a high table with stools that's angled to face the screen. I give a wave to my dad, standing in the corner with a huge bowl of food.

Once everyone is seated, Mom stands up on top of her stool, which elicits a growl from my dad. "Emma, be careful."

"Relax, Thatchy. I'm taking a picture for Wes to send to Cara." She taps at her phone a few times and I hear the camera sound. "She should know she's got a cheering squad."

"USA! USA!" Odin and Wyatt start chanting as the national team appears on the screen, arms linked on the sideline as the national anthem starts. Warmth spreads through me when I see Cara, who has her eyes closed as she sings along. She seems calm, which is great because I know she'll be amazing out there. She's worked really hard for this.

"Wesley, are you going to send her the photo?" Mom leans over the table behind me.

"Not during the game, Mom. She doesn't have her phone on her right now anyway."

"Which one is she?" Gunnar squints at the screen when the camera pans to the full field after the Jamaican anthem.

"False nine." Uncle Hawk surprises me with his awareness of Cara's new position. He shrugs when I glance over to him. "Lucy's been getting updates from Akemi."

"This whole thing must be so difficult for Lucy." Aunt Alice rests her head on my Uncle Tim's shoulder. He grunts in response but doesn't say anything. "Tim, I know you're not allowed to talk about it, but can you at least—"

"Ssshhh!" Wyatt waves a hand as the match kicks off. I'm relieved that my family, with so many serious athletes among us, knows when to hush up if it matters.

My bowl of chili sits forgotten in my lap as I stare at Cara. The new position puts her in the center of the field, and it seems like every other pass comes right to her. She moves the ball so accurately, sending perfectly timed passes to the forwards. The US dominates the field from the first whistle, and it feels like only seconds pass before Cara has a break-away. She feints right and moves left and then, swish. I imagine I can hear the net ripping from the force of her goal.

"What a cannon!" Wyatt springs to his feet, pumping his fist. My other cousins all start chanting "USA, USA" and I'm not going to lie. It feels amazing knowing my family is this excited about the success of someone I care about.

A few minutes later, Cara intercepts a pass and lets loose a long ball that shouldn't go into the net, but the Jamaican keeper misjudges the angle and the ball sails right in past her glove. Mom leans forward again to say, "Oh, Wesley, she's wonderful." Mom ruffles my hair and I lean back into her hand, catching sight of Dad out of the corner of my eye. He's smiling.

The rest of the game goes by in a blur of refilled bowls, cheering, and zero goals from Jamaica. We're down to injury time when I see an unmistakable streak of dark hair in the center of the screen. Cara sprints, seemingly out of nowhere, to intercept a pass and nobody can catch her as she charges right for the goal. Her new position puts her in exactly the right place to make these sorts of moves.

She shifts her weight, fools a defender, and spins past another. Stopping to plant her foot, Cara swings and snaps the ball into the corner of the net. I'm on my feet screaming, barely registering my mom yelling, "I can't see! I want to see the replay."

"Emma, stop standing on the damn stool. You'll break your neck." Dad strides over to her and must intervene because Mom's red mop of curls starts bouncing in my line of vision. I don't need to see the replay. The series of moves is burned into my brain. My girl is incredible.

My girl.

"A tremendous display of talent from the young Pittsburgher," the announcer is yelling above the crowd in the stadium. My family eventually calms down. People start washing dishes the second the ref blows the final whistle, but I stay where I am because I want to see as much of Cara as they'll show on the television. Thankfully, my family knows to wait a bit before they start teasing me about her.

The camera pans along the players as they shake hands, and the US captain preps for an on-field interview as she swaps jerseys with the Jamaican captain.

I lean forward to look for Cara, milling around in the background with the rest of the team, exchanging hugs, bouncing, clapping hands. Everyone seems impatient to congratulate her and she accepts all the praise graciously, smiling brightly and turning to face each well-wisher.

Then I see a guy I know she won't be happy to greet. Lou Rubeo walks onto the field, shaking hands with all the US players. I grit my teeth, understanding that this is part of his job as president of the organization. But...I must be hallucinating because I swear, I see him approach Cara and spin her around to face him.

And then I swear I see him grab her face with both his hands and kiss her on the mouth.

My Cara.

This man has his lips on her on international television. Her body stiffens. I see her arms go rigid. He's gone as swiftly as he arrived, shaking hands with staff from the Jamaican team. Like he didn't just assault my girl.

I can't breathe. I imagined that, right? As the camera pans away from Cara, I just about convince myself that the whole thing was a messed up illusion, until Wyatt snaps off the television and shouts above the chaos. "What the actual fuck was that?"

I look around and my entire family is silent, mouths open in shock and disbelief. It was real. That actually happened.

I yank at my hair and then I have to get out of there. I sprint from the room and out the front door before I can register who is yelling my name.

CHAPTER 20
CARA

I BARELY MAKE it to the trashcan in time before I puke up water and bile. My body violently heaves, screaming at me from the inside. The burn in my esophagus grounds me as reality sinks in: Lou Rubeo just grabbed me and kissed me on the mouth, in front of 20,000 fans and an internationally televised audience.

"Cara!" Jay's voice breaks through the fog as I grip the edges of the trash barrel in the tunnel leading to the locker room. I turn my head toward her voice and see her face etched with concern.

She places a hand on my back as one final retch takes over my body. "Come on, friend. Let's get you in the locker room."

The press starts rushing to the tunnel, heels clacking on the polished concrete. I don't know how many of them saw what happened or if they're just excited about the outcome of the match. It's hard to tell what's real. Rubeo just moved on from what happened like it hadn't happened at all, and nobody pulled him aside or dragged him away.

As soon as Jay guides me into the locker room I sink onto a bench and rest my head against the wall. Coach Akemi bursts through the door and skids over to me on her knees. "I just heard what happened. Cara! My god. Where is your agent?"

"My agent?" My eyes feel swollen and it's hard to see individual faces from the crowd now hovering around me. I haven't talked to my agent in a few weeks. I'm still too new for endorsement deals. I'm not sure how she would respond to her client being grabbed and kissed against her will. Is that even something the rest of the world cares about?

Coach Akemi places a reassuring hand on my shoulder. "They're going to want a statement from you, honey."

"Who? Who is they?"

Coach waves a hand around. "Everyone? Soccer USA. The Olympic committee. The World Association Football Union. The press …"

"What is there to say?" Jay hands me a bottle of water and I start chugging. She pulls the bottle back.

"Easy there, bud. Go slow so you don't puke it up again."

A male voice slips through the crack in the swinging doors to the locker room. "Everyone decent in there? We've got a hungry press corps out here, gals."

I don't recognize the voice, but it doesn't seem to matter. Coach bellows back, "We're all naked. Tell them to wait." She returns her gaze to me, eyes serious. "Cara, I want you to go into the coaching offices and call your agent. She'll answer, I promise." Coach stands up and looks around the room. "Hogan, get Moreno's phone from her locker and throw it over here, please."

My teammates have all been standing around staring, silently, as this interaction unfolds. Hogan shakes herself and heads for the shelf in my locker, extracting my phone. "You're blowing up, Cara."

I nod and take the phone from her, seeing countless notifications. My hands shake as I bring myself to my feet and I notice my thumb scrolls over a message from Wes.

Holy shit! That's incredible. I can't wait to watch.

My stomach drops further, if that's even possible. Wes was watching. He saw another man kiss me. My legs tremble as I walk to Coach's office, worried he'll once again think I sought out that behavior from Rubeo.

Worried he'll think I liked it.

Worried Wes will see it as a rejection of him. Tears roll down my cheeks as I remember our night together before I left for training camp.

I sip water slowly, preparing to look for Alex Steele's number, but my phone rings and it's her calling me anyway. "Hello?" My voice sounds like, well it sounds like I just vomited stomach acid.

"Soccer USA just called me, babe. They want a statement."

Alex doesn't have time for small talk. She told me that when Coach Lucy first gave me her number, and I haven't minded before, but now I really need some context. "I don't know what that means."

Alex sighs. "It means they're going to want you to say *boys will be boys*."

I freeze and try to ignore the spiders I sense crawling on my skin. "That's not what happened."

"Anyone with a brain can tell that. Hell, social media even seems to agree you looked terrified, and the internet doesn't agree on anything."

"It's online already?"

"Oh, lady. Do me a favor and turn off all your notifications. No. Have your roommate do it. Are you alone right now?"

I tell her Coach sent me into her office, presumably so she could deal with the media. I do hear quite a ruckus out in the locker room.

"Soccer USA plans to say Rubeo was 'caught up in the

moment' of your decisive victory and couldn't contain his joy about your tremendous talent blah blah bullshit blah."

I forgot that I scored a hat trick, my first since high school. For a second, a bit of calm settles over me and I almost smile. And then Alex keeps speaking. "They're going to want you to confirm that you, too, were overjoyed and happy to share in that proud moment."

"That's not what happened."

Another sigh. "I know, and I'm going to tell them that. But I don't need to tell you what it's like for a woman to work in the sports industry." I purse my lips. "Total fucking sausage factory, Cara. You should assume everything you're assuming is accurate."

"Well, it sucks. I'm just...trying to make America look good on the soccer field."

"I know. Do you want to sleep on it? Which I recognize is a bullshit phrase because I doubt you'll sleep tonight."

She agrees to tell the organization that I need time to draft a response. I hide in Coach's office for a long time, staring at a gray metal cabinet until Jay comes in to tell me the media has left.

She waits for me while I shower and change. By the time we get on the team bus, the mood is joyful. People are celebrating our victory and someone hands me a paper cup of champagne.

Hogan smashes a button on a bluetooth speaker and Queen's "We Are the Champions" blasts throughout the bus. It's easy to shove down my agony about what happened after the match, especially as everyone around me seems so focused on what happened in the 90 minutes we spent working together on that field.

I let my body dance down the aisle and toss back the champagne, accepting high fives as the team chants "golden boot! Golden boot!"

We pull into the hotel parking lot a few minutes later and

the team heads straight to the hotel bar, everyone piling duffel bags in the lobby, forgotten like the weight of what happened to me.

Coach Akemi waves for me to come over to her. She holds out her phone, brow furrowed. "Is this what your agent agreed to?"

I see a social media post from Soccer USA, predictably stating that Rubeo was caught up in the moment…but I also see a quote presumably from me, where I supposedly said, "we were all overcome with excitement. These things happen."

CHAPTER 21
WES

BE *Careful When Enjoying Women's Sports*
By Ed Realm, News and Views

Give Us a Kiss, Then: Did Cara Moreno Invite Affection?
By Karen Jones, Liberty First Online

Is the New Generation of Female Athletes Asking Too Much?
By Tom Edwards, Bros, Balls and Banter

Cara isn't taking my calls. I know she and Jay are back in Pittsburgh because I asked my Aunt Lucy. I've sent what I hope are compassionate messages to Cara. I even sent flowers to her apartment with a note about how I'm thinking of her and on her side no matter what.

I know in my bones that she never said "these things happen" about that monster assaulting her. I've seen how upset she was for months after he just touched her face. There's no way she's not suffering from being grabbed like that in what should have been an overwhelmingly joyful cele-bration of her talent.

I decide to linger at the stadium after the Forge training this morning, since I know Hot Metal is doing off-season workouts in the afternoon. But I must miss Cara's arrival because eventually I hear the sounds of the team taking the field.

Determined to make contact with Cara, I go grab some lunch and hurry back to the stadium to meet her after the workouts. Armed with chicken salad, grapes, and a pumpkin tart, I position myself right outside the locker room. And then I wait.

At first I scroll social media, but I opt against that as I see more headlines from fuckers making it sound like Cara is making a big deal out of nothing.

The locker room door creaks open and I straighten, expec-tantly. No Cara. Jay sees me, though, and walks over. "Hey, Stag."

"Jay. Is she in there?"

She shakes her head. "Dude, I'm concerned. She went back to the weight room after we finished sprints. She's going to burn herself out in more ways than one if she keeps this up."

My shoulders sink at this news. "Does my aunt know she's doing extra workouts? Isn't that frowned upon?"

Jay shrugs. "Lucy knows. She's in there with her."

"Oh hell, my uncle is going to flip out."

Jay nods. "Already happening, Stag."

I hold out my container of chicken salad toward Jay, whose eyes light up. "Here, you take this. I'll go see if I can do anything."

She shouts after me as I walk toward the weight room. "You're welcome to try."

I can hear my uncle bellowing in frustration.

"Lucy, you're 45 years old. Do you really want to blow out

your ACL over this?"

I hear feet pounding and the treadmill whirring. When I open the door, I see my aunt in a full-out sprint, barely sweating, staring straight ahead as she runs. Cara matches her stride for stride, also ignoring my uncle, who paces the room while tugging at his gray-streaked hair. "If I didn't think you two would trip and fall, I'd unplug those machines. God damn it, where is Tim?"

As if summoned by the universe, my uncle appears behind me, straightening his tie, several underlings in line behind him. "Lucy, Cara." Tim tilts his head, his expression demanding attention be paid. My aunt flicks a button on her treadmill and hops to the side rail as it slows to a stop. Cara follows suit. Neither of them are even breathing heavy as they straighten out their shirts and stare at my uncle. Nobody seems to have noticed me yet, so I lean against the back wall.

"Yes. Well. Here's how things stand." My uncle waves a hand toward a colleague, who hands him a piece of paper. "Soccer USA is holding firm to their 'boys will be boys' statement. Alex Steele has been quite clear that Cara never approved the statement they attributed to her." Uncle Tim hands the paper back to his colleague and folds his hands in front of his waist, looking down from his impressive height at Cara and Lucy while my Uncle Hawk grinds his teeth. "Right now, our choices are to go along with these statements—"

"Absolutely not. No fucking way." Uncle Hawk throws his arms in the air. "Lucy was fired from the national team for bringing up this guy's bad behavior and then he escalates to televised assault? No."

"Thank you, Hawk, for summarizing the problem." Uncle Tim keeps his gaze trained on Cara as he scolds his brother for interrupting. "Cara, my firm and I cannot represent you in this matter because it's a conflict of interest. We are employed by the Hot Metal, who are a franchise member of Soccer USA."

Cara looks like she is going to hyperventilate, but Aunt Lucy squeezes her hand reassuringly. Tim gestures toward a woman near the back of the room and I see my Aunt Lucy sag in relief and recognition. "Cara, this is my friend Tawnya Kimani, partner at Jones, Lynch, and Kimani. *She* has enthusiastically offered to take your case."

"My case?" Cara looks confused and I want so badly to cross the room and offer her a reassuring hug.

Aunt Lucy wraps her arms around Tawnya and I remember that they're old friends. Wyatt grew up hanging out with Tawnya's twin sons. "Hey," I pipe in from the back of the room. Everyone turns to look at me like they're just now realizing I'm here. "Doesn't Tawnya's husband own the Forge? Isn't that a conflict of interest, too?"

Tim shakes his head. "At this stage we don't believe so. Tawnya will draft a letter seeking disciplinary action against Rubeo, as well as an accurate statement from Cara about what happened."

"About what happened to Lucy, too, right?"

Everyone stares at me for a few moments before turning their heads toward Aunt Lucy. She stands up straighter and adjusts her shirt collar. "I'd like to focus on what happened to Cara but am prepared to join into the calls for disciplinary action if needed."

That statement seems to set the legal people into action, and they don't really seem to need input from anyone else at the moment, which doesn't stop my Uncle Hawk from following them into the hallway, shouting about the nonprofit organization he started to help fund legal support for women who have been abused.

Abused. The word hangs in the air until Cara and I are the only ones left in the weight room. She stares at me, and I can tell that the next words from my mouth will either drive her to collapse or give her the strength to walk out of here in one piece.

I swallow and pull up the bag from the deli. I clear my throat. "I brought you lunch. I'd offer to eat with you, but I gave mine to Jay and it's long gone."

I watch Cara's face melt into relieved contentment. "Thank you," she whispers, taking the bag from me and sinking onto a weight bench. I perch on the end, not sure if she wants me close enough to touch her, but hoping she might. I miss the feel of her in my arms, the solid, strong weight of her.

"This is really good, Wes. Do you want to share it with me?"

I wave a hand at her. "I'll get something at home. You need your strength." I don't say that she needs it for the brewing lawsuit and media circus. I also don't say that she needs it as she keeps preparing her body to compete in the Olympics.

She wolfs down a few bites before slowing to stir the chicken salad, glancing over at me. I edge a bit closer to her and she seems to relax even more. "Wes, I'm so tired."

"I bet you are. Jet lag and all." I nudge her with my shoulder and smile. Thankfully she returns the expression a bit.

"I could really use a distraction from all this." She waves her hand toward the hall, where the lawyers are still conferring. By which I mean shouting.

I look back to Cara, fighting the urge to touch her, to run my fingers through her hair. "Have you thought any more about talking to someone about what happened?"

She growls and I know I've said the wrong thing. "All I do is talk and talk about what happened. Nobody even asks about my hat trick. They just want to know when I got so close to Rubeo. Close!"

I clench my abs and my legs to avoid exploding at the thought of him being close to her in any capacity. "I just want to make sure you have the help you need, that's all."

"What I need, Wesley, is someone to help me feel good for a few minutes so I can refill my tank. God, you're acting just like you always say your parents act when you're injured. Like it's the only thing you're allowed to talk or think about. Ever." She shoves the bag of food at me and stands. "I wasn't asking you to fuck me. I was just hoping we could hang out."

She stomps toward the door in a frenzy of dark curls. "Cara, wait, I'm sorry. You're right, okay?"

She slows but doesn't turn around. She mutters something and I lean closer, trying to hear. "Can you say that again?"

When she turns, the fire has dimmed in her eyes and she looks vulnerable, biting her lip and looking up at me. "Where do we stand?"

"What do you mean?" My heart rate picks up and I place a hand on the wall for support.

She swallows and I love staring at her body carrying out those basic functions. Every part of her is amazing. I should tell her that. But she says, "Asking you to kiss me before ... it drove a wedge between us. And I want to be closer to you again, Wes."

I can't help the smile that tugs on my lips at her words. "I want to be close to you, too." It's the biggest understatement of my life, like saying Pittsburgh has a few bridges. "I'd love to hang out with you and, I don't know. Eat seaweed snacks."

She shakes her head. "Those taste like a fart."

I smile, feeling a sliver of hope. "I'll think of something we can do that smells nice."

Her face shifts into something not smiling exactly, but no longer miserable or angry. With a curt nod, she strides out of the weight room and over to her new legal counsel.

CHAPTER 22
CARA

SOCCER SWEETHEART CALLS *Foul Over Post-Match Smooch*
  By Ken Benton, Celeb Spectator

Romance or Rude? Sources Reveal Months-long Flirtation Between Soccer Star and Organization President
  By Nick Alders, A-List Almanac

Did Soccer Prez Cross a Line?
  By Tom Edwards, Bros, Balls and Banter

I haven't slept in a week. Between the jet lag, the media, and the stress of having to relive months of discomfort, I just can't get my brain to turn off. I know I look like shit. I know I'm playing like shit.

I keep hoping this next thing will be the one that lets me unclench and just ... pass out.

"Cara, mi niña, you need to take some time off and get

some rest." Rosalie's accent thickens when she worries, so the sound of her voice really tells me I look worse than I thought. "This fucking guy accusing you of lying is bananas. I've seen the video."

"I don't want to talk about the video. Please." I massage my temples as I lie on the couch with my phone propped on my lap, my friends' faces tiny squares of encouragement in a world increasingly full of people wanting to analyze my life.

"Okay," Shante pipes in. "Well, I read the new statement you put out. I mean, who hasn't?"

Toni shakes a finger in the air. "It's all over socials."

I bang my head against the arm rest a few times. "All of it is all over socials. That's the problem. I can't think. I can't even brush my hair without someone analyzing my intentions."

The newest layer of this scandal is Rubeo claiming the kiss was mutual. Nobody seems to remember that he was going with "caught up in the moment" as his non-apology. Now it's all a huge discussion about how I flirted my way into a starting position on the national team.

Rosalie frowns. "I'm going to start posting more screen shots of your goals in that match. Like…you scored *three* sick-ass goals. How is anyone curious about how you got picked to start?"

Shante sniffs. "God forbid someone just punish a man for doing something wrong."

I sigh. "Hey, chicas, I love you. But I can't talk about this anymore today."

Toni squints at her screen. "It's only 10."

"Exactly."

"Okay, Cara. We'll let you go so you can rest."

Seriously? My best friends can't talk to me about something other than my international scandal? They're hanging up? I wave in frustration and end the call as Jay shuffles down the hall from her room.

"I take it you're not coming in today?" She talks around a bite of breakfast muffin, and I realize I haven't taken my turn cooking. Or cleaning. I glance around the apartment and see the piles of junk mail and dirty laundry on every surface.

I groan and, instead of getting up, sink further into the couch.

"I'm glad you're taking some time, Cara. Don't worry about the apartment. We'll get to it." Her pep talk is interrupted by a knock at the door, and I lift my head to see Wes giving Jay a high five as they pass one another on the threshold.

He wrinkles his nose and sniffs. "And you accused my snacks of smelling like fart?"

I throw a pillow at him. "Shut up. It does not smell like farts in here. It's just …"

He grins. "I'm kidding. But I did think of something we could do that will smell nice."

"I'm not really in the mood to go out in public right now." I gesture at my disheveled state.

Wes walks around to the couch and lifts my feet, sliding his body under my heels and lowering my feet back to his lap. He starts rubbing my feet through my socks and I groan out loud, both from the friendly, familiar contact and because it feels sinfully good. "What if I told you it wasn't public? I set up something private. Just you and me and the person working there."

"Working where?" I close my eyes as Wes switches feet, pressing his knuckles into my arch. His fingers are strong and the pressure is perfect. I briefly wonder if he'll go into massage therapy when he stops playing pro, but I don't want to think about Wes's future. I want to bask in the delicious contact right now.

"Working at the surprise, fragrant date place I set up for us today."

"It's a date?" My eyes fly open.

He scrunches his face in adorable confusion. "I mean … isn't it a date any time we hang out? I thought … we were … dating …"

He sounds so uncertain, so concerned. A wave of discomfort pulses up the back of my scalp. "I hadn't thought about naming it. Everything is so confusing for me right now. God, everything I do is under a microscope."

"Hey!" He drops my foot and rubs a palm up my leg. "I'm sorry. You're right. We don't have to name anything, okay? But I did set up a special … appointment for us and I'd love to take you if you're up for it."

I bite my lip. "I really should clean up the apartment before Jay gets home."

Wes rubs a palm along his cheek and looks around. "It's not so bad. I'll help."

"What? No way. I can't ask you to do that."

He shrugs and pops to his feet. "I offered. Come on." He extends a hand toward me and, frowning, I take it and he hauls me to my feet.

"Don't lift me! Your back."

"How about you let me worry about my back and you sort through the mail while I get the dishwasher going?"

He doesn't wait for me to argue, but walks over to the sink and starts rinsing things, loading up our dishwasher like he has a masters degree in plate arrangement. My mother would be both impressed by his technique and confused about why a man would be touching a dirty dish.

I watch him work as I quickly shuffle through the mail, recycling most of it and setting aside two small piles of important stuff for Jay and me. Wes is still scraping oatmeal bowls when I finish, so I gather up the laundry and get the washer going. By the time I pull my head out of the front loader, he's got a broom in his hand and hums as he dances around my kitchen, sweeping.

"Are you singing 'Dancing Queen' while you sweep my floor?"

He hums louder, passing the broomstick from one hand to another. "In my head it's 'soccer scene.' I'm digging the soccer scene, get it?"

I can't help the laugh that escapes my mouth. "You're ridiculous."

"Hear the shout of the refereeeeeeeee, oh yeahhhh. You can kick. You can slide. Kicking the goal of your liiiiiife."

Wes drops the broom and grabs my hand, twirling me around the kitchen as he croons made up lyrics. I laugh at him, each word from his mouth more ridiculous than the last, until he runs out of ideas. "You ready for our appointment?"

I sigh. "I guess I am. Thank you."

He leans in and kisses me on the cheek. "You're welcome."

————

Wes heads toward his neighborhood in his giant car, which I now realize he needs so his head isn't banging the ceiling. Every part of him is long and lean, and my cheeks heat as I remember a particularly long part of him I haven't seen in a long time.

He parks along the curb on Butler Street and I glance up, not familiar with this block of the bustling neighborhood. There are a bunch of bars and little restaurants with every type of cuisine, it seems, apart from Spanish … or Cuban, of course. Longing for my mother's cooking burbles up in me, palpable. I nearly sob but I reach for the door just as Wes opens it, his hand extended to help me out of the car.

I realize I'm in a trendy neighborhood in old sweats, with no makeup and uncombed hair. I stiffen, until Wes leans in and says, "You look perfect. We're wearing practically the same outfit." He grins and runs his hands down his hoodie. I hadn't noticed that his black and gold sweatshirt reads Hot Metal instead of Pittsburgh Forge.

"You're wearing women's soccer gear?"

He pats his chest. "I'm a huge fan. Have you seen their midfield?" He fans himself and I give him a shove.

He guides me toward a building with a very busy font on the sign so I can't make out the name. Something mix … and we walk inside to a wave of fragrance.

"Wes! Welcome. And this must be Cara." A sales clerk, whose name tag reads Alanna, approaches with a wave. "I'm so excited to do a custom pour with you both today."

"A what now?" I glance around the shelves and realize Wes brought me to a make-your-own candle shop. The walls are lined with hundreds of jars and scents, and it all combines to a lovely, fresh aroma. Alanna lowers the window shades, giving us privacy, and I glance around. "This is so nice."

Alanna nods. "Why don't you two have a seat and we can get an idea of what sort of candle you'd like to create."

Wes hops up on a stool and immediately says, "I'm making one for a very special woman who hates the smell of seaweed but always makes me think about water."

"Water?" Alanna and I speak at the same time, but he keeps his gaze on her and nods.

"Yeah. She gets into this flow state when she's working, and she's powerful and she sparkles. And she can be very dark and stormy."

Alanna smiles. "She sounds very special. Why don't you try some of these scents and see if any jump out at you." Alanna puts a tray of tiny bottles on the table in front of Wes, with labels like solar lily and bergamot.

She turns her gaze on me. "Are you looking for any specific mood? What scent profile are you thinking about?"

I try to name some of the things I'm feeling about Wes right now, but all that comes to mind is "gratitude. I am just feeling really grateful for my candle recipient."

Alanna smiles. "We can work with that, most definitely." She sets a wooden tray in front of me, and I start sniffing tiny vials, distracted by Wes enthusiastically inhaling and following each sniff with a loud "aaah. Nice."

Eventually, I pull out sandalwood, cedar, and something called labdanum. Alanna seems delighted by my choices and turns toward Wes. "Are you thinking of using them all?"

He shrugs. "It all smells really good."

"That would be a very complex scent indeed."

Wes grins. "Well, that's perfect, Alanna, because this person is very complex." Alanna nods and gestures toward a selection of jars, telling us to select a home for our candle creation while she gets the essential oils ready to mix into the hot wax.

I consider Wes for a few moments and then choose a smooth black jar. He spins around with a white jar in his hand, grinning. I notice a leaping deer painted on the jar— probably a reindeer for Christmas, but I let him have his moment of joy because it's adorable.

We return to the table and Alanna set us up with wax and wicks and tiny spoons to add our scents. As we work on the candles, I focus on the feel of Wes's leg pressed against mine, the joy on his face as he continues to inhale the tiny bottles of fragrance. I asked him to take me somewhere and take my mind off my troubles, and I would have never imagined pouring candles would tick that box.

"I'm calling mine Big Wick Energy," Wes says, sliding his complete candle to the edge of the table. "It's to remind my recipient of me."

I swat his arm. "You're bad."

He leans in to whisper in my ear, "No, Cara, I'm very, very good for you." And then he kisses my neck, and the pleasure of it sets my hands shaking. I dump a bit more sandalwood than I intended into the candle, and I decide to quit while it's still salvageable.

"Mine's called Don't Blow It." I smile at Alanna, who nods. Wes and I have the option to create professional-looking labels for our candles and we spend some time choosing ridiculous fonts. I can tell Alanna thinks we are goofballs, but honestly, it's such a relief to do something frivolous that I don't care what she thinks.

We get our labels stuck on our candles at last and Alanna explains that they need to set for at least two hours. "You can come back for them this afternoon, or any time this week if that works better."

"Thank you so much for your help," Wes says, fishing some cash from his wallet.

I pat my sweats, looking for my own money, but Alanna shakes her head. "Mr. Stag pre-paid for your session. But thank you, so much, for the generous gratuity." She nods her head toward Wes, who gives her a wink.

"You ready to get out of here, Moreno? We've got time to fill!"

———

Wes suggests we hang out at his place since it's only a few blocks away, and we move his car to his building so he can stop feeding the meter outside the candle place.

Except, when we get in his car, the radio comes on and it's a news report. "… today as the president of Soccer USA faces temporary suspension. A spokesperson from the organization declined further comment, mentioning an ongoing investigation into a personnel issue."

Wes lifts his hand to shut it off, but I grab his wrist. "No, wait, I want to hear this."

"…from within the soccer community claim Rubeo assaulted national team player Cara Moreno, allegedly grabbing her, and kissing her on the mouth without consent after a US victory over Jamaica. Tawnya Kimani, legal representation for Moreno, says more details will continue to unfold, and that her firm is prepared to pursue legal action."

Wes frowns and pulls into the garage at his building. "Legal action can mean all sorts of things."

"Shh."

"—meanwhile, sources close to Rubeo continue to assert that Moreno had been flirting with the soccer executive for months. They released a video of the soccer starlet celebrating after the match with her team, drinking champagne and allegedly unaffected by any form of alleged assault. To see the video and learn more about this story, visit our website at WBNA dot—"

Wes yanks his keys from the ignition, cutting off the radio. "A fucking video of you happy? Like you can't be happy about winning and still furious at ...what he did?"

I swallow and step out of the car, walking slowly toward the elevator. "I really need to sit down."

"Of course. Sorry. Here I come." He clicks his key fob to lock the car and waves a different fob to summon the elevator. He stands opposite me in the lift, concern etched into his features. I stare at his neck, seeing tendons flex as he swallows and grinds his teeth together. His anger grounds me in reality, lets me believe I really am seeing and hearing all this nonsense about someone from my place of work behaving criminally and then denying it.

The elevator reaches Wes's floor and he steps out, unlocking the sliding door to his loft. "Can I get you some water?"

I should prop myself on a stool at his counter or sink into the couch in his living room, but I don't. I follow him over to the sink. "Wes, I need you."

"I'm here, Cara."

He turns to face me, but I shove him back against the counter. "No, I need you to fuck me."

"What? Cara—"

I shake my head and place my palms on his chest. "I need to be in control. I need to choose. I need to feel so god-damned good because I want to, despite what anyone else says. I need to know if I still can. Do you want me?"

He swallows again, eyes wide. "I wanted you from the moment you first yelled at me at that airport. But—"

I place a finger over his lips. "No buts. I need you. Right now."

CHAPTER 23
WES

I'M SO CONFLICTED. The hottest woman in the world is shoving me against my own sink and telling me to fuck her. But this woman has also been through a lot and just got out of the car listening to radio announcers discuss her like a social studies topic. That has to be messing with her head.

The last thing I want to do is give her something else to regret. "Cara." I swallow, trying to hold back the fear that what I feel for her is too big, too strong. "I...can't go all in like this and then lose you again."

I know it's not fair to bring up my own worries while hers are so big and so present. But I also can't give her what she needs without letting go of the control over my emotions—the last thing I have keeping me safe.

"I need *you*, Wes. Please. I'm not going anywhere."

Cara grabs my palm and presses it to her chest. I feel her nipples pebble through all the layers of her sweatshirt. She's been pretty clear for a few weeks that she wants this—it's been me putting on the breaks, insisting that she should want me for me, not as a distraction from what's hard in her life.

But she didn't ask me to take her mind off things just now.

She asked me to give her control and choice. *"I need to feel good,"* she'd said. She grabs my other hand and presses it to her crotch. I feel the damp heat of her body and a groan escapes my throat. I growl and pull her against me. "You want to be in control, baby?"

She nods her head rapidly. "Yes."

"Tell me what you want." I lick my lips, waiting.

She smiles, a slow, spreading expression that slides over her face like a mask of happiness. Soon enough, I'll help her find that joy more permanently. For now, if she wants this, I'm going to give it to her. "Go lie on your bed." She tilts her head toward my room. "Take your clothes off as you walk."

I do as she says, and I risk a glance over my shoulder to see her following suit. We shed our sweats in a heap of fuzzy black and gold. I wonder if I should pause to pull off my socks, but Cara comes up behind me and I feel her nipples against the middle of my back.

I turn at the doorway and walk backward towards the bed and tip onto the mattress just in time to catch her above me. She straddles my waist, her heat against my thighs as her palms slide down my chest.

She seems to consider her next move, and I make my hands busy while she ponders. "Can I touch you?"

"Everywhere," she nods, pinching my nipples.

I gasp. "Fuck, Cara." My dick twitches in response to her rough touch and she reaches for it, thankfully with a more forgiving grip. She fists my cock as I tease her thighs, touching her lower belly, everywhere except the ball of nerves I know she's hoping for.

She moans in frustration. "I want to …"

"What, baby? Anything."

Her eyes flare, wide and dark. "I want to sit on your face."

"Oh, fuck, please. Yes. God." My head sinks into the pillow and I rest my hands on her golden hips as she makes her way up my body. I smell her, more potent and wonderful than anything in that candle shop, and as Cara grips my headboard, I inhale long and deep before she lowers herself on my eager tongue.

"Please, Wes." I lick her gladly, my hands digging into her rounded backside. The familiarity of her body, of her taste, tugs at my memory like warm sunshine. I play with her clit using my nose and my mouth together while my hands gently rest on her butt and she rocks back and forth, groaning.

"Oooh, yes. Just like that. Harder, now. Faster." Cara barks out commands and I follow like an eager soldier. I'm incredibly turned on at the sight of her dark hair spilling over her shoulders, her brown nipples bobbing as she jerks and shudders above my face.

I'm greedy for her orgasm, realizing I need to give it to her as much as she needs to claim it. "Come for me, Cara." I nudge her with my nose as I encourage her. "Be a good girl and come on my face."

I readjust my grip so I can slide my thumbs along her seam while I hold her over me. She sinks into place in my palms and both my thumbs slide inside her body just as she tumbles over the edge, an orgasm ripping through her as she pulses around my hands and tongue.

She grunts and thrashes, finally tipping to the side, panting. I roll to face her, grinning. We could stop right here, and I'd die a happy man, knowing I gave that to her. But Cara Moreno has no intention of stopping.

She shoves me onto my back again and climbs back aboard, this time tracing a fingertip along my ribs. She teases the sensitive skin from my belly to the root of my cock. "I haven't been with anyone since you, in California." She brushes her hair back, revealing a serious expression. We both know we're tested frequently at work, but I like that she's telling me this.

I shake my head. "Haven't either. No one but you." My breath comes in bursts as she starts playing with my dick, her grip the perfect pressure as she slides up and down my length.

"I'm on birth control. Monophasic hormone levels are supposed to help prevent ligament damage and—"

"I get it. You want to ride me bare." My mouth hooks in a crooked grin. The thought of sliding inside her, nothing between us, nearly has me spurting in her hand. "Yes. I'm so good with that. So, so—oh shit."

Cara lowers herself onto my shaft and we groan in unison at the sensation. I've never felt anything like this in my life. She is wet velvet inside, so slippery. More than that, I can feel the trust between us right now. There is nothing separating us with me inside her and that knowledge grips at my heart so tightly I whimper. I stare down at our joined bodies as she starts to rock herself above me. "Cara." Her name is a whisper, a prayer of gratitude.

But I remember that this is about her and what she needs. She grabs for my hands again, pulling them to her chest and I gladly play with her tits while she uses her hands to find the leverage she needs. Cara is on the brink of coming a second time without any assist from me.

I'm doing as I was silently told, stroking her nipples and pulling, pinching those hard little berries while she gets herself off on the friction of our pelvises rubbing together. "So … fucking … good," she hisses, and then I about blow my load when I see her reach between her own legs, finding the exact pressure she needs to cross the finish line.

"Oh, shit, Cara, I'm going to come." I give her about a second of warning before I blast off inside her, watching in awe as she melts above me. Her face is such a perfect picture of bliss, of joy and pleasure. I spurt again as I realize I helped her get there.

After I grab us some warm washcloths from the bathroom,

I haul Cara into my arms and play with her hair until her breathing slows and I realize she's fallen asleep. Remembering the dark circles under her eyes when I first got to her apartment, I decide to hold her and keep her safe as long as she needs to rest.

CHAPTER 24
CARA

You are so exquisitely beautiful

Do you like my Big Wick Energy?

HE TEXTS me these things every few hours and it never fails to put a smile on my face, even with everything going on at work. I need to continually remind myself that soccer is my job, that this is my professional work and 99 percent of the people at my workplace treat me as I would expect to be treated at work.

I light the candle he made me every afternoon when I get home, and I've made a habit of sitting and sort of staring at the flame, organizing my thoughts after my shower. It's like meditation, I guess. I never tried it before.

Most evenings I have stressful calls with my agent about the latest spin from the national soccer association. I didn't necessarily want Rubeo fired in the beginning. I'm not sure what I wanted … just for him to go away and leave me alone.

But I've come to realize that as long as he stays in the position of president, I'll continue to see him at every training camp, every international fixture. There's no way I could go to the Olympic Games and be expected to sit near him at a press conference about our team unity and pride for our nation.

Alex Steele is enraged that the board for Soccer USA won't fire Rubeo, so now in addition to getting him fired, she's urging me to make a plea to replace the patriarchal board of directors, too. "Nothing is going to change if we don't get rid of the people making excuses for abusers." Alex's anger and firm words make me feel like my own anger is okay. So, I take her advice at every turn.

Which is why I'm already geared up for a fight when my phone rings, but it's not my agent this time. Or my lawyer. It's my mother.

"Cara, I have Papi on speaker. We're outside the church."

"I didn't think you guys went to church anymore." I suppose we've skipped over the part where we pretend to greet each other with love and affection.

"Don't be profane. Of course we go to church." My father scolds me like he hasn't spent the past two decades of Sundays watching any professional soccer match fielding a player of Cuban descent.

I inhale and stare at my candle flame, thinking of Wes.

"Cara, what's all this in the news about you luring this man?"

"Mama, I hope you know I'm not luring anyone. I hope you think more highly of me than that." I clench my fists and concentrate on the candle, which sputters a bit with my breath. I sit back so I don't accidentally blow out the flame.

My father roars. "How dare he touch you? On television! How dare that man lay hands on a woman like that."

"We didn't have these problems with you at the girls' schools. This is why we were so worried about you at that college, going around with all these men. These men don't know how to behave themselves." I can hear my mother crossing herself, probably sitting on a bench near my father, perhaps ignoring the fact that they're sitting outside a church that doesn't allow divorce at all, let alone an amicable one like they had.

"I'm glad you can see that the man is the one with the problem here, Mama. I was just trying to do my job ... and honor my country." I add this last bit with a false hope that my father will chime in with one of his usual declarations about the impact of Cuban Americans on our economy.

Instead, he sighs. "We think you need to come home. You still have a room at your mother's apartment, and one at mine. You aren't safe there with those men."

I stare at the candle, thinking of Wes, thinking of how my experience here has led to me being named a starting player on the U.S. Olympic soccer team. My heart breaks that my parents don't seem to care about either of these accomplishments. They see only what the reporters suggest: that I somehow brought on Rubeo's attention by being a woman.

I take a stuttering breath. "I have to go now, Mama, Papi. I will keep you updated on my travel schedule. I hope you can still plan to come see the friendly match in Chicago."

I hang up before my father can reiterate that it's a long drive as the weather gets colder. A tear slides down my face and I flick it away, hearing a small hiss as the drop hits my Big Wick Energy flame.

———

"Knock, knock." Jay pokes her head in my room. I still haven't gotten into the habit of closing my door. I spend a lot of time thinking about how many years it's been drilled into me that it's always, always my responsibility to ward off the uncontrolled sexual urges of men. And any sexual urges I might have myself.

I remember how I felt on top of Wes the other day, how

powerful and happy and strong. I remember the look of sheer delight on Wesley's face as he brought me to climax, and I can't believe I ever let anyone tell me it's not okay to want that experience.

I brush my hair off my face and smile at my roommate. "Hey. What's up?"

She purses her lips. "I know you turned off all your notifications and took all the social media apps off your phone."

I nod. I was getting inundated with direct messages from angry people. *It's just a kiss. We can't even kiss women now?* And those were the things from the nicer people. Jay volunteered to scan social media on my behalf and give me a summary if there was anything my agent or lawyer needed to know.

I should buy her a candle or something for that labor because I sure as hell can't handle that work.

"Well, I wanted you to see some of the stuff. Just some of it. Hogan and I copy-pasted some highlights."

"Hogan?"

Jay smiles and nods. "A lot of the Hot Metal keep asking how they can help, what they can do, all that sort of thing. Well, here." She hands me a piece of computer paper with a bunch of tiny screen shots pasted to it.

He's always been creepy to me, too. Used to stare at my boobs at press conferences. #WeStandWithCara

Rubeo is a criminal abuser. Touched my ass once—uninvited. #WeStandWithCara

Nobody should have to deal with that abuse at work. And soccer is work. #WeStandWithCara

Current and former members of the national team all seem to be posting similar sentiments about Lou Rubeo. It seems like none of them ever thought it was bad enough to say something, but so, so many women felt uncomfortable around him, avoided being alone with him, or worse.

"Jay, this is … I don't know what to say."

She sits next to me on my bed and pulls me in for a hug. "You don't have to say anything because you already said the thing. And we believe you, Cara. Everyone who matters believes you."

Jay smacks a kiss on my cheek, and I burrow into her shoulder, feeling lucky to have been assigned her as my roommate all those months ago. I never thought I'd feel a connection with someone as intense and powerful as I had with my friends from college, but I'm starting to see that the women's soccer community is full of like-minded people.

"Anyway," Jay loosens her vice grip. "Does that candle say Big Wick Energy?"

I nod. She rolls her eyes. "Straight people are weird."

———

Jay heads out with Hogan and the defense, leaving me alone in the apartment with my feelings. So of course, my mind wanders to Wes.

We still haven't circled back to a conversation about our status. Are we dating? Does what we have defy labels? Either way, I'm eager to show him the print-out from Jay and tell him about my new hashtag.

When I check my phone, I see a note from him that he decided to take advantage of open hours in the weight room at the stadium.

I can drive down there and surprise him, and maybe he will invite me back to his loft for a remix of our adventures from the other day.

I deliberately avoid the radio as I drive to the stadium, letting the messages Jay showed me replay in my head instead to give me encouragement while I drive. We stand with Cara. Every woman on that curated list said the same thing: they stand with me.

I'm practically floating through the door, the green light

from my badge flashing brightly in the dimly lit hall. I can hear the clang of weights and I'm sort of glad Wes is still here working out. He told me he's been killing it in scrimmages. I guess outrage gives him an edge. Or maybe it's the fumes of that candle I made him.

He catches my eye in the mirror as I round the corner into the weight room and his gaze darkens immediately. He's shirtless, glistening with sweat, bursting through a set of thrusters with a heavy barbell and plates.

His body is chiseled perfection. Every tiny muscle in between all his larger ones is flexed as he works the weight up and over his head. Wes grunts with the effort of the movement even as he maintains eye contact through the mirror. I lean against the back wall of the room, incredibly aroused at the sight of him.

He bends over to drop the bar, his bubble butt popped back in my direction, draped in mesh shorts that end midway up his tight thighs. Wes growls as he picks the bar up again and heaves it into the air, straightening to his full height and looking like da Vinci's Vitruvian Man sketch. My eyes drop to his crotch and sure enough, his bulge moves, seems to swell.

And then I yelp as Wes drops the weight to the ground. He turns and stalks toward me, his intention clear. He's a Stag ready to rut and I am ready for his horns. I giggle at my ridiculous analogy until he gets near me. I can practically smell the lust on him. It turns me on a lot.

Wes boxes me in against the wall, one forearm on either side of my face. "When did you get here?"

"Just now." I reach out and rest a hand on his sweaty chest, liking the feel of his heart racing beneath his skin.

"Did you find what you were looking for?" Wes tilts his head to the side, breathing heavily from his workout. Or maybe he, like me, is dizzy with desire right now.

"Not quite." I reach for his mouth with my thumb,

intending to rub his lower lip, but he snaps his jaws and sucks my thumb into his mouth.

Wes releases my thumb with a pop and studies me, considering. Wordlessly, he presses off the wall and starts toward the door, extending a hand for me, which I take.

He tugs me into the men's locker room, gives a quick look around, and nods as he strides toward the shower. "I'm filthy, Cara. You have to know that."

I swallow and nod. "I can see that."

He grins. "And you like that, don't you? You like it when I fuck you dirty." I nod, watching as he drops the shorts to the ground and kicks off his sneakers. "Get naked, now, or I'm going to throw you in there with your clothes on."

I hurry to comply, excited by his rough words. We haven't had this kind of sex since California—this inevitable, horny sort of coupling that's rough and kinky and delicious. A breath after I peel off my last sock, Wes has me backed against the tile in one of the locker room stalls. There's no curtain, but I also know there's nobody else around and I release a moan as he dives in to begin sucking my nipples in the hot spray of the water.

Steam from the water forms a cloud in the shower stall, softening the sting of the harsh fluorescent overhead light. I peer through the mist at the dark head and gray eyes of Wesley Stag, who sinks to his knees and wedges my thighs apart. He grunts as he squeezes my thigh and hooks it over one of his shoulders before he dives in and starts licking my center like it's the last phase of his cardio workout.

I sink into the tile, my hands resting on his messy, damp hair as I let the pleasure overtake me. This is what I need. I need the way he understands me, knows what I want and likes what makes me feel good.

And there is no question he likes this. Wes moans with pleasure and reaches between his own legs to fist his cock while he pulls me closer and closer to the cliff with his tongue.

"Oh god. Damn, that feels good. I need you." My words come in short bursts with long moans in between and then I'm coming on his mouth while I feel his dick bopping me in the ankle as he works it furiously with his fist.

I thrash around in the shower stall as he brings himself to his feet, still rubbing at his erection. I move to reciprocate, not caring that he hasn't washed himself off yet, but Wes shakes his head. "I won't last, Cara. And I want to come inside you."

I swallow, my stomach turning flips and my legs still shaking in the aftershocks of the orgasm he just delivered. All I can do is nod before I'm hoisted from the ground. Wes rests my butt on the small shelf meant for toiletries, and before I can protest that my weight will break it off the wall, he nudges in between my legs and thrusts inside me. He holds my thighs with his strong hands, the shelf just taking a bit of my weight as he begins to fuck me hard.

My spine digs into the tile and I hear the combined sounds of our grunts, our skin slapping, and then a low, keening wail I realize is coming from my throat as Wes releases one of my legs to reach for my clit.

"Wes! Wes! Yes, please keep doing that." I grip his shoulders, slippery and swaying, as he pulls a second orgasm from me.

I feel his hairy thighs against the back of mine as he lifts my legs higher, hooking my ankles over his shoulders. He's so deep inside me now, the tip of his cock bumping my cervix and causing me to bear down on him.

"Oh, fuck, you're so tight, baby. You like when I'm fucking you this deep?" I nod my head and he grins wickedly, moving his hand from my clit and massaging lower, further back.

He finds the tight pucker of my ass and I remember how he started to play with it when we were together in California. I'm running out of energy now, sure he's fucked the breath out of my body, but a jolt of molten steel warms my entire body as Wes pokes the tip of his little finger inside my most private place.

I come apart in his arms, and I hear him growling that he's coming, too. I feel the pulsing surges of it, the warmth inside me, and I hear him purring into my ear. "You're so beautiful, Cara. So fucking hot and perfect right now. Christ, look at you. Look at you." I glance down and I can see myself spread around him. His wrist is angled beneath one thigh, and I can feel his finger still inside my channel, which grips him tight like my heart.

"Take me home, Wes."

He nods and kisses my temple. I rest against the wall of the shower while he soaps up his hands and gently washes my body, then his own. We dress quickly and head towards his place.

We hold hands walking back to his room, like teenagers on a date, and I love the freedom and silliness of that. I wake up in his bed, tucked tight against his side, feeling safer than ever before.

CHAPTER 25
WES

KISS-GATE AT WOMEN'S *Soccer Friendly*
  By Ken Benton, Celeb Spectator

Outcry Over Post-Match Celebration
  By Amanda Peters, Fame Frenzy Online

Cancel Culture Comes for Celebrating: Can we even show excitement anymore?
  By Nick Alders, A-List Almanac

My uncle, in coach-mode, texted the entire team to let us know there's increased security at the stadium for the time being. Even though it's the off-season, and the pro teams don't have mandatory workouts yet, there have been a ton of paparazzi hanging out trying to take pictures of Cara.

I received a special, bonus series of texts from my entire family warning me to keep my cool and let the lawyers handle everything, no matter what these guys say.

It's not easy.

If you had told me I'd spend the tail end of my first pro season injured and then removing social media from my phone because I can't handle the trolls coming after my girlfriend, I'd have laughed in your face.

Girlfriend.

Cara hasn't used that word, and I haven't pushed her again for a label. I want to trust my gut on us, that we are in a good place together. She spends almost every night in my bed, curled up in my arms. And that's better than any sort of label.

———

Cara and Jay had a special strategy video call with their coach from the national team, so she stayed at her place last night. Instead of waking up to have lazy sex, I drag myself out of bed to head in for cardio and weight training.

I see the light flashing off what looks like a thousand camera lenses as I approach the gate to the parking lot. During business hours, the stadium parking lot is used by commuters who mostly work downtown, so there's no real way to keep the media out of the lot as long as they pay their parking fee.

Something tells me they're happy to drop $20 per van so they can swarm the gates, begging anyone who walks by to talk to them just for a minute. I keep my head down and my hood up as I shuffle past them, eager to connect with the security guard nodding me toward the player entrance.

"Thanks, man," I say, offering a hand to the guard to jostles me through the reporters all asking my name, if I know Cara Moreno, if I ever got "carried away" after a soccer game.

"You got it, Wes." The guard shakes my hand and I feel guilty that he knows my name and I have no idea who he is.

But then I remember I'm a pro athlete in a city that worships its sports teams.

"Hey, man, let me know if you ever want an autograph or anything." I realize it sounds a bit desperate as I say it. I'm a rookie nobody who only played in one match, after all, but the guy's face brightens.

"That would be great! Me and my old man are tracking your whole family. We got a Ty Stag rookie jersey, signed, from when he started with the Fury."

"That's awesome. I'll make sure and grab something for you, okay?"

He gives me a salute and I make my way into the locker room, reminding myself that there are still good people out there in sports fandom. Not everyone is chomping at the bit, eager to tear down the players.

"We can't fucking do anything anymore." I hear the voices of my teammates in the locker room, shouting about something.

I make my way to the bench by my stuff and start wedging my bag in the narrow, vertical space. "Tell me about it." The guy on my left, Harrison I think, kicks at a roll of tape on the ground. "One of those fuckers shoved a camera lens right in my face. Almost chipped my tooth."

I grunt. That's aggressive and unnecessary. "They shouldn't behave that way."

Harrison nods. "All because some chick can't handle a kiss." He throws a shoe into his cubby, but I freeze where I stand.

"What did you say?" My words come out sounding harsh, but I mean for them to cut glass.

Harrison looks at me. "I said some fucking chick can't handle a little celebration kiss and now we all live in a police state."

I wait a beat, sure some other guys on the team will speak up. Will say something in Cara's defense. Will decry the slime ball who grabbed her against her will. But nobody does.

And all the frustration, all the rage I've felt for months ever since I realized this guy was making her uncomfortable to start with? It all flies out of me through my fists as I shove Harrison up against the wall, screaming and bashing his shoulders off the divider between our two storage shelves.

"What the fuck, man?" Harrison tries to get a punch in to my ribs but I grab him by the shirt and spin him so we're standing on opposite sides of the bench. I duck my shoulder and move to dump tackle him like my football-playing cousins taught me.

All the years of growing up with a brother and eight male cousins come to a head as I transfer decades of horseplay into an outlet for my fury. I dig a knuckle into Harrison's sternum, a knee into his thigh as I swing.

He gets a punch in on my jaw but I barely feel it, pummeling him with both hands as I straddle his body on the sticky floor of the locker room. I'm screaming, shrieking with rage when I feel a pair of hands lift me off Harrison and I finally realize my uncle is in my face yelling my name.

I snap my mouth shut and drop my hands to my sides. Uncle Hawk is breathing heavy and gives me a shake. "In my office, Wesley. Now! Harrison, come back in an hour. Bring your agent. We're going to talk about your morality clause."

My uncle keeps a hand on my shoulder, steering me toward his door while he mutters about asshole men who don't get it.

"Did you hear what he said?" I sink into a chair and press the heel of my hand into my eye. It's throbbing. Harrison must have popped me in the face more than once.

"Yeah, of course I fucking heard him and half the team saying things that, frankly, upset me a great deal. I was in the middle of arranging a training about intimate partner violence prevention when you went ballistic and took it into your own hands." He swipes a hand along his desk, scattering pencils and post-it notes. "Which I expressly told you not to do, Wesley."

I wince. Between the pain in my face and the sting of his words, I'm starting to feel like a real heap of garbage. "So, what happens now?"

He leans on the edge of his desk with his arms crossed and brings one hand up to massage his graying temples. Uncle Hawk takes a deep breath. "Now you go and see a psychologist, Wes."

"What?" I recoil. "You're sending me to a shrink?"

He glares at me. "Shrink? Seriously?" He shakes his head. "Look, I know you know this, but your aunt was going through some crap when we first met. She and Wyatt went to counseling for a long time, and it wasn't until I finally did, too, that I was able to let go of some of my own anger about the whole situation."

I rub my face, mirroring his action, but wincing in pain. "I didn't know that you were in therapy."

"Hell, kid, everyone needs therapy. Which is why we have a psychologist on call, ready to work with all the athletes in this program. I would hope people would take advantage of that gift voluntarily, but now I'm going to mandate you attend as a condition of you returning to my active roster."

"You can't do that."

"The hell I can't!" He kicks the leg of my chair. "Don't mess with me on this, Wes. Get your ass up to Doctor Georgia and get your head on straight." He stalks toward the door and pulls it open before stopping and turning toward me. "Cara needs you at your best. This is going to get uglier before it gets better."

He strides out of the room, yelling orders at the guys as he heads to the field, where I guess I won't be joining him today.

CHAPTER 26
CARA

"YOU CAN'T GET RID *of me that easily." Soccer USA Pres will not resign.*
  By Ed Realm, News and Views

Not Fired: Lou Rubeo and the Kiss Nobody Cared About
  By Ken Benton, Celeb Spectator

Board Says Rubeo Can Stay: Soccer organization president prepares for Olympic Games in Paris, hopes to put misunderstanding behind and come together as a nation.
  By Tom Edwards, Bros, Balls and Banter

Jay growls as I enter the kitchen. I can't get ahold of Wes and was up half the night worried something happened to him. I considered messaging his cousin Wyatt, but I chickened out.

"What's up, roomie?"

"Fucking Rubeo. I know I'm curating the news for you,

but his *mother* is on a *hunger strike* and is hospitalized. She's refusing to eat until his name is cleared."

"What?"

Jay nods. "I'm dead serious. She won't stop until the world stops besmirching her son's good name."

I swallow a knot of bile, wondering if it's possible to puke from disgust. I've already vomited from exertion and, after the last USA match, from trauma and fear. What's a little revulsion retching? "His mother thinks I'm lying?"

Jay growls and punches the couch cushions. "Bae, a lot of people say you're lying."

I grip the edge of the counter, frozen in the middle of the room. "But the hashtag…"

Jay sighs. "Come on, let's sit and come up with a plan here. Because yes. There is a hashtag. There are people supporting the shit out of you, but there are also a fuck-ton of people making it all worse."

Jay and I already decided to arrange our training in another location since there's been so many paparazzi at the stadium. The studio where Wes and I took yoga for athletes has a bunch of workout space that Jay and I have been using to follow Coach Akemi's workouts for the national team.

Jay microwaves a pair of egg muffins and I choke one down as she drives us to Pipe Fitters. I like the atmosphere, with brightly colored walls painted with positive affirmations, and I come close to enjoying myself during the workout. But each time my stomach pings with a well-earned hunger, I think of Lou Rubeo's mother, refusing to nourish herself until I … what? Say the kiss was consensual?

Indicate that it's normal and fine for someone to grab me at work and kiss me without permission? I'm back into a rage before the final set of kettlebell moves. "I can't handle this, Jay. I can't handle any of this."

She heaves a weighted ball into the air, aiming for a spot

high on the wall. "You can and you are. It just sucks, Cara." She grunts and throws the ball again, and I decide to join her even though this isn't on my workout plan. It's cathartic, hurling a heavy ball into the air and sinking into a squat as I catch it.

When we finally head home, I'm ravenous and almost okay about that, mentally. I whip up a giant bowl of tuna salad and prop my feet on the coffee table, connecting my phone to the television screen so I can call my chicas and see them on a bigger canvas.

"Cara, querida. I'm taking Twitter off my phone." Shante snaps her fingers in rage as she frowns.

"Twitter isn't even a thing anymore anyway." Rosalie waves at me but then frowns as well. "But I know what you mean. All this bullshit. When do you have to go back? Will he be there?"

"What do you mean?" Toni is eating actual popcorn as she settles in for our call. She's still wearing her lab coat, and I smile, thinking of her as a lead investigator on her own research study already.

Shante rolls her eyes. "Cara is gonna have to go back to California with the national team. You know—to get ready for the Olympics? And that monster is in charge of the whole sport sooooo, you know. He'll be there, right?"

The hand holding a forkload of tuna stops midway to my mouth. I drop it into the dish. I had not stopped to think that if Lou Rubeo isn't fired and the board won't suspend him, then of course he'll be present at camp. He'll be carrying on his work like it's any old day of the week.

Shante squints at me. "Cara? You okay, chica?"

I shake my head. "I … didn't stop to think that he'd be at camp."

Jay comes into the room fresh from her shower. She waves at the camera and my friends blow her kisses. "You didn't think who would be at camp?"

Rosie snorts. "This fuckwad with the mama on a hunger strike, that's who."

Jay's eyes widen. "Oh, shit. You're right."

I grip the arms of the couch. "We leave in a week."

"What's your lawyer say? Hang on. Someone's at the door." She walks over to the intercom and squints at the image, then pushes the button. "It's your reindeer." She sits on the arm of the couch. "Has your lawyer said anything? Or Alex Steele?" Jay turns to the screen and addresses my friends. "Did you know she's my agent, too?"

"Good for you, girl." Rosalie smiles briefly, then her face slips back into rage mode. "Cara, what *did* Alex Steele say about this?"

My mouth opens and closes a few times but then Wes bursts through the door to my apartment and I see from the corner of my eye that he has a massive shiner. "Wes?"

The tuna bowl clatters to the floor as I spring out of the couch. "What happened?"

He waves a hand and saunters over to the couch. "It's nothing. I just … can I come sit with you for a little?"

Shante, Toni, and Rosalie are literally leaning into the camera as if they can get closer to Wes and examine his face as I'm doing. I gently trace the outline of his bruising. "This isn't nothing. What happened?"

"You want some ice?" Jay talks around a mouth crammed with tuna salad. She must have picked my bowl up from the floor and helped herself.

Wes shakes his head. "I took an elbow to the face during a scrimmage, that's all."

Jay arches a brow at him and swallows her food. "Must have been one hell of a corner kick if elbows were flying that hard. Your keeper okay?"

Wes waves a hand and then turns to face my friends. "You must be the beloved Midfield Mamis."

"Oh, we are." Shante nods. "I've heard about you, Wes Stag. I know where you live, and I know who your family is."

He snorts. "Most people know who my family is."

Shante makes a sound like "mm hmm," and shrugs. "Well, I don't have time to tell you that if you hurt this woman, I'm going to wax your pubic hair and feed it to you."

"My god." Wes claps his thighs together and I slide closer to him on the couch, making room for Jay, who still has my tuna.

I'm grateful for the chaotic distraction until Rosalie shakes her head and groans. "Wesley Stag, you did not get that in a scrimmage. You were in a brawl."

"What?" Jay, Toni, Shante, and I yell in unison as we all turn to face Wes, who closes his eyes.

"Some of the guys were upset about the added security at the stadium. You know, for the paparazzi."

"So? I'm upset about it, too." Jay tosses the empty food bowl on the coffee table and crosses her arms over her chest.

Wes takes a deep breath. "Well, one of the guys said something I'd rather not repeat about the Rubeo incident. And I lost my temper."

My friends all start shouting that they're glad he stood up for me like that, how they hope he taught that guy a lesson. All I can hear is that my worst moment has infiltrated the locker room of the men's team here in Pittsburgh and that someone very important to me feels the need to violently defend my right to exist without being grabbed.

"I can't do this." I say the words quietly and repeat them more decisively.

"Can't do what, sweetie?" Rosalie mimics petting my hair like she used to do in person if something upsetting happened.

"I can't go to the camp. I have to boycott. If they won't fire Lou Rubeo, I won't play."

The room is silent for a few beats and Wes grabs my hand,

squeezing. Jay drapes an arm around my shoulder and hands me my phone. "You better call Alex. She'll want a heads up, or maybe she will be the one to call Akemi."

Wes nods and keeps on squeezing my hand. "Maybe call Tawnya, too? You'll probably need a lawyer since this is a contract issue."

I take a deep breath, preparing myself to make these calls, feeling calmer than I have for weeks. I'm not going to just casually give up my dreams, obviously, but I feel a sudden certainty that this is the way forward, that boycotting and refusing to play, refusing to score goals for the United States, is the way to get them to listen when I say I won't be treated like that.

Jay springs to her feet. "If you call Tawnya, ask her for a referral for me, too."

"You, why?" Wes chuckles. "You gonna beat someone up?"

"No, asshat. I'm boycotting the national team, too." She rests a hand on my shoulder. "If you're not going to camp, I'm not going. We have to get rid of this guy. Together."

CHAPTER 27
WES

I DON'T KNOW what to wear to therapy. On television, whenever someone's in therapy they seem like they stop on their lunch break from an office job. My office is a soccer field, and I'm not allowed on it until I deal with this, so I go with a polo shirt and black jogging pants.

I knock on Dr. Georgia's door and pull at my collar as I wait uncomfortably in the hall. The door opens, revealing a short woman with dark skin and a wide smile. "Wesley Stag! Good to meet you. Come on in." She opens the door and gestures into her office, which is painted yellow and manages to capture the gray Pittsburgh light and make it seem sunny.

"Call me Wes, please."

She nods and sinks into an armchair. She has a small desk in one corner, but the rest of the room is filled with different types of furniture. There's a massage table along one wall, a couch, and a wingback chair opposite hers. "Sit anywhere you like."

I nod and perch at the edge of the wingback.

She smiles and clicks her pen. "Your coach asked me to talk with you about the altercation in the locker room. But I'd like to start by just checking on how you're doing overall."

I scratch my head. "What do you mean?"

She shrugs. "How have the last few months been for you? Your medical records indicate you've had quite a comeback from an injury."

I shrug. "Parts have been great. I'm playing pro soccer, right?"

She nods. "You are indeed." And then she waits.

And I wait, and I realize I'm supposed to keep talking. "So, yeah, I had the injury and that sucked. But my girlfriend was really supportive while I was in physical therapy."

"It's wonderful to find someone who supports us when we're ill or injured." Dr. Georgia smiles. I try to decide if it's cheating if I don't go back and say the word girlfriend is presumptuous of me. Dr. Georgia continues. "Getting injured must have been disappointing, especially so early in your career."

I nod. "Disappointing. Yeah."

She taps her lip. "Is that what led to the fight in the locker room?"

A swell of anger pulses behind my ribs. "I think you probably know that the fight was about my girlfriend, who was assaulted on television, and Harrison said some fucked up things about it."

Dr. Georgia squints and does that slow nod thing. I hated it when my parents used to do it, and I'm not thrilled to see now. "My notes from the coaching staff indicate that you and Ms. Moreno are, perhaps, quietly dating, and also that Mr. Harrison made rude remarks, prompting the coaches to arrange for some intimate partner violence prevention education, and that you took issue with the remarks and physically attacked your teammate. Does that sound right?"

"Yes!" I growl the answer, because it is accurate but also so inadequate, I'm not sure what else to even say about it.

I stand and start pacing the office as Dr. Georgia keeps nodding. "You clearly care very deeply for this woman."

"Cara."

"Okay. Cara. My understanding is that she experienced harassment and you..." she gestures like I'm supposed to keep going. I don't know what to say. Dr. Georgia sighs. "You haven't been able to directly intervene. What's that like for you?"

I yank on my hair. "It's utterly infuriating, that's what it's like."

"Tell me more about that, Wes."

I roll my eyes and sink back into the chair. "She's worked so hard and she's so fucking amazing. Like, top of the world amazing. Unparalleled. And then she's dealing with this nonsense, and I can't do a thing about it. I can't protect her. I can't even get my own teammates to see why it's wrong for men to treat people that way. Like, how dare this small-ass guy make her feel powerless."

"Mmm. Yes. I see." Dr. Georgia nods.

"Sure, you see. The people who see, see. But I have no clue how to make this type of thing stop. Not a damn clue. I'm so angry."

"I can see that." Dr. Georgia starts taking notes on her pad of paper. Who even knows what she's writing down. I realize I've been shouting, and half the stadium probably heard me bellowing. I take a deep breath.

"You know, Wes, it's admirable that you want to defend Cara." She smiles. "But you also must know you can't control others' actions. What you can control is being there for her, supporting her in constructive ways. Managing your own reactions."

I have my mouth open to tell her I am supporting Cara. I'm distracting her, I'm giving her what she needs. But I'm not managing my own reactions to anything. Not really. I snap my mouth closed.

Dr. Georgia clicks her pen again. "Many people who experience harassment feel powerless to stop it. And the people who love those experiencing harassment feel those same overwhelming emotions."

"I spend a lot of time imagining what it would be like to fly out there and throttle this guy."

Dr. Georgia says, "hm," and writes something else down in her notebook. "The desire to take action is understandable. Are you maybe making an assumption about what Cara needs, though?"

I grind my teeth together. "Cara needs to boycott the national team. She told me that yesterday and then asked me to go home so she could sleep alone."

"And that didn't feel good."

"Of course it didn't. She's my fucking girlfriend." Except that's not all of it. If I'm brutally honest, I feel a little guilty because I used to be some guy like Harrison, who saw Rubeo with Cara and didn't recognize how harmful his actions were.

Now, after what we've shared, I feel like Cara is mine, body and soul. And I think that might be the crux of my rage right now. This Rubeo fucker messed with something that's mine.

Dr. Georgia raises her brows and gestures for me to go on. "Do you feel like boycotting isn't enough? That you should do something in addition to her choice?"

I stare out the window. Dr. Georgia's office has an excellent view of the freight trains going opposite directions along the banks of the Mon River. "I guess I feel ineffective."

"Hmm. Sort of like when you hurt your back?"

I stare at her. I breathe for a few minutes and nod. "Yeah. Like that."

She clasps her hands in her lap. "It sounds like you have a bit of a tendency to downplay your feelings, whether physical or emotional. Does that seem fair?"

I shrug. "I have no idea. You're the expert."

"Well," she starts. "What happened with your injury?

How did you process those big feelings about something so important?"

I snort. "First I had to get my parents to stop wailing that I'll wind up paralyzed."

"Your parents?"

I wave a hand. "Yeah. I hurt my back before, in high school, and my dad laid into me that I'm going to wind up in a wheelchair unable to take care of myself."

"That must have been extremely frustrating to hear on top of your disappointment at getting injured."

"Yeah. Okay. I'm sensing a theme."

She smiles. "And that is?"

I tap my fingers on the arm of the chair. "I hate feeling like I can't do enough, and then I hate it more when other people tell me not to do more, and it all just simmers."

"And then what happens?" She arches one brow expertly, and I briefly wonder if that skill is a prerequisite for becoming a therapist.

I sigh. "I snap." I think about my snap judgment when I first saw Cara with Rubeo in California, how I immediately assumed something awful. I think about screaming at my parents and eventually just not even telling them I was going to the elite camp to be seen by scouts. I think about tackling Harrison to the floor, and I decide he deserved that beating and I'm not going to waste more energy dwelling on that one.

Dr. Georgia sets her notebook on the floor next to her chair and leans forward. "We are out of time for today. But you made some insightful connections here about how you respond when you feel powerless or ineffective. I'd like to work with you to build some healthier strategies to process your emotions if you're up to that."

I nod. "I guess. What happens now?"

She smiles. "Now you go home, and we meet again next week, same time."

CHAPTER 28
CARA

WOMEN'S NATIONAL *Team Gets Emotional in the Face of Moreno Accusations*
   By Ed Realm, News and Views

Since When Is a Kiss Such a Problem: Can women stand up to competition on the field if they can't handle the celebration afterward?
   By Logan Henderson, A-List Almanac

Within minutes of Jay texting the rest of the players named to the national team, they all decide to boycott the camp in solidarity. A few of them even message me privately that they, too, had had uncomfortable interactions with Lou Rubeo. None of the players will agree to play until the organization fires him.

I have absolutely no idea what to do with that collective support and break down crying on the floor of the apartment until Jay calls Coach Lucy, who drives over to sit with me. She runs her fingers through my sweaty hair and doesn't say anything, just lets me cry out loud until my throat hurts.

"It's hard to process a big wave of love when you're used to a fight," she soothes. And then she starts to tell me about her ex, a man who manipulated her and made her feel small and eventually started stalking her. "The hardest thing for me at that time was accepting help from my soccer team … and from Hawk." She smiles as she says her husband's name, a far-off look in her eye.

Lucy takes a deep breath. "I would be remiss as your coach if I didn't encourage you to speak with a mental health professional about all of this." I stiffen. I know instinctively that therapy is good for everyone, and I've done a lot of work with the team and the sports psychologist, blinky eyes and all. But I didn't grow up in a family that encouraged me to talk about my feelings, and I certainly never had anyone in a position of power tell me that someone else is to blame for anything that happened to me.

Lucy continues, her hands still soothing me. "I can see why you might not want to speak with someone associated with the team, Cara. But I met some terrific professionals at the women's center, and I'd be happy to make a recommendation."

I sniff. So far, Lucy's recommendations have a 100% record of being amazing. My agent, who Lucy found for me, is actually flying in later today to talk more about the national women's team boycott. I draw in a breath and manage to sit up. Lucy hands me some water, which I sip gratefully. "I'd like that. If you could suggest someone to talk to." I bite my lip. "But I don't know where to start …"

Jay lets out a relieved sound and I remember that she's still here, draped over the back of the couch, concerned. "I've been to tons of therapy," she tells us. "It's great for my game, not that I'm playing right now. But anyway, just let the doc guide the conversation if you're stuck. Want me to drive you to a session?"

———

A few hours and a long shower later, I'm nestled into a comfy couch in a brightly lit therapist's office not far from Jay's and my apartment. Apparently professional athletes can get in to see professionals on the fly ... that or Lucy called in big favors. The therapist is a Middle Eastern woman who told me to call her Amira. She smiles from an overstuffed chair across from me, her silver bob haircut glinting in the sunlight. "I read the notes your coach sent over, as well as the information from your intake form. Cara, that must be very difficult. How are you doing today?"

I shrug. "Not great? I don't know what to say."

Amira nods. "You must have worked very hard for a very long time to be selected for the national soccer team. Can you tell me about your soccer career?"

My eyebrows shoot up into my hairline. "My career might be over just as it's getting started." Amira waits patiently for me to elaborate. "I just feel like I'm always that little girl, begging the grownups to just be allowed to play. And they're always telling me I'm just a little girl who shouldn't want to."

Amira sits forward in her chair, elbows on her knees. "Can you tell me more about that? Who are the other grownups invalidating your talent?"

I roll my eyes. "My whole life. Everyone. My parents ... they wanted me to be a timid little princess in skirts, on the hunt for a husband. Now this fucking guy thinks all I'm good for is his sexual pleasure. Or something." A wave of nausea forces its way up my throat, and I cough into my fist to avoid vomiting at the thought of Rubeo's mouth against mine. I reach for a water glass on the table by the couch.

"Take your time." Amira nods and just waits. She really is a good listener. I take a few breaths to gather my thoughts.

"I just want to play soccer. I don't want to be a femme fatale out to get men fired. I don't want to be an icon. I just want to go to work, train hard, and play with my team. I've earned that."

Amira nods. "You certainly have. You are a tremendous athlete. Your coaches are unanimous in that assessment."

I grunt. Amira leans back in her chair. "Unfortunately, what you are experiencing is common for women in all career paths, and you're certainly in the limelight in a high visibility career like athletics." She leans forward again. "But this harassment and abuse does not erase your talent. You have accomplished so much, despite these obstacles."

I don't know what to say in response to that, so I just stare at her. She smiles and a few beats pass. I can't tell if she's waiting for me to say something else, so I just sip the water and stare at her.

"I worry I brought this all on myself."

Amira frowns. "Can you tell me more about that? I want to understand what you mean."

I tap at the arm of the couch, thinking about my parents, the shitty referees I used to have in high school who viewed officiating a women's game as a punishment. "It's like no matter how good I am, there are always all these people trying to undermine me. All the women's players. Like we're a joke or something."

Amira nods. "Not a funny joke, is it?"

I shrug. "Eventually it just feels like maybe I don't deserve to be here. Or maybe I do deserve … whatever Rubeo is doing. Like that's the cost of playing."

Amira nods empathetically. She seems to nod a lot. "You did nothing to deserve being harassed and mistreated. The blame lies entirely with the perpetrator and those who allow him to remain in his position. Not you."

I stare at her.

"Let me repeat that, Cara. Because it's very common for people who have had these experiences to blame themselves. But this is not your fault. You did nothing wrong."

I blink a few times and turn away from her gaze. "I feel stupid for hoping I could just play soccer. Like ... my boyfriend just plays soccer. He gets up and goes to work and gets a bigger paycheck than me and nobody thinks he's being cute. I guess it was naive to think I could have that, too."

Amira nods a few times more and taps the arms of her own chair, studying me. "It's not naive to expect fair and equal treatment. You deserve to feel safe and respected. This is in no way your fault."

The more she says that the stiffer I feel. Like a big ball of fire is crawling up my spine and squeezing my throat. It's very hard to believe her, to believe I've earned the right to my place among the soccer greats when so many others see me as an object. Jay has tried to keep me from the headlines and the comments online, but I've seen what people are saying. I've heard the names they're calling me.

Amira continues. "My office is a safe space for you to process unfair treatment. Whatever you feel is the right thing, and the only way through all this is to honor those feelings and try to understand them."

I swallow through the sludge of overwhelm. Amira smiles at me. "I'm so proud to have met you. You are a resilient, talented person."

The tears come again, and I let them. Amira sits quietly, patiently, while I cry. Afterward, I feel both empty and full.

CHAPTER 29
WES

I FEEL DRAINED after therapy and all I want to do is take a nap, preferably with Cara in my arms. I figure she must be pretty overwhelmed, too, so I stop and grab us some food and head toward her apartment to see if I can convince her to take a siesta with me.

I raise my hand to ring the buzzer, but Jay flies out the building door and I grab hold of it. "Hey." I hold it open for her as she squeezes out.

"Oh. Stag. Hey. She's up there." Jay smiles. "She'll be glad you're here, I think."

And then she bustles off, shouting for her phone to send a message for her and growling when the robot voice seems to misunderstand her commands. I saw some of the headlines. I know the women's team decided to boycott their camp this coming weekend unless the national office fires her abuser.

I clench my fists against the flame of rage licking my throat at the thought of this guy. I try to remember that Dr. Georgia said this is normal. It's normal for me to feel angry like this. I just have to learn what to fucking do about it other than smash someone's face.

I take the stairs up to Cara's apartment two at a time and

tap on her door. She pads over to it, and it sounds like she's wearing slippers or something. I'm staring down at the floor when she opens the door, so I see the leopard print fuzzy footwear before I glance up and see her face. "Cara." Her eyes are puffy and it's obvious she's been crying. I open my arms and she steps right in and I squeeze her tight.

Her scent wafts around me, like a fog of calm. I just feel right when I'm with her. I don't know that anyone else has ever understood me the way she has, and I don't know that I've ever known anyone else like I do her. She doesn't have to tell me she's feeling overwhelmed by her teammates stepping to bat for her. It's no light lift to get a group of women to put their professional sports careers on the line like this.

"I saw the news," I whisper, and she nods against my chest. "Want to take a nap?"

She pulls her head back a few inches to look at my face. "Is that a euphemism or do you really want to sleep?"

I smile. "I want whatever you want…" She frowns. "Okay, I want to actually sleep. But I'm game for whatever in a few hours if you let me hold you."

A sigh slips out and she seems to melt into me even more. I'm feeling pretty good, pain wise, and I stoop to grab her legs with one hand, hooking her up in my arms with a smile on my face. "Feels good to haul you around."

She reaches around and pats my back. "It doesn't hurt anything?"

I shake my head. "I'll tell you if it does."

A few short strides later and I'm placing her gently on the mattress. Cara has said before that she's got some weird hang-ups about doors being open, so I reach for it and catch her eye. She nods and I push it shut with a snick. Then I kick off my shower slides and crawl into bed with her, plucking the slippers from her feet and tucking her against my side.

"What did I miss?"

"Hmm." I love drawing sighs from her. I love making her

feel good. She is such a fierce lioness. I have no doubt she could eviscerate anyone, mentally or physically, if she set her mind to it. And I get to hold her in my arms. "I saw a therapist ..."

"Me, too," I whisper, kissing her ear.

"That shit is hard work."

I nod and squeeze the fingers she has laced through mine around her belly. I feel her drifting off, the slowing of her breath as she sinks into the mattress. The warm lure of sleep sneaks up on me ... until my phone rings.

And it's the special, obnoxious ring I set up for my agent at his insistence. Cara groans and I roll away from her, reaching for the phone to quickly answer so the noise stops. "Hello?" I whisper in a way I hope conveys my irritation. Because what the fuck, man. It's the off season and he knows I just went to my mandated therapy session.

"Wes, baby." Brian has a way of talking to me like I'm simultaneously five years old and the most important person in his life. "I've got news."

"News you couldn't text me?" I wedge the phone under my shoulder and turn sideways, needing to touch Cara to ground myself. I rest a hand on the swell of her hip and wait.

"So, I know you're aware that the Olympics are coming up."

"Yeah. No shit."

"Don't talk to me like that, baby. I'm your daddy here."

"Brian, do not ever call yourself that again or I swear to god I will fire you."

"Fine, fine." He chuckles. "Did you see Lewis blew out his knee at camp this week?"

"What?" The starting left wing for the national team has been to three World Cups. I have a signed photo of him and my Uncle Hawk on the field together before Hawk retired.

Brian grunts. "Bad tackle at practice. Shitty timing for him and the team and all that."

I pull my hand from Cara's butt and drag my fingers through my hair. "That really sucks, man. Thank you for telling me personally, I guess."

"Wes. Baby. Beautiful, obtuse baby. Lewis is out and they need to replace him. They're calling up players to the training camp this weekend before the friendly match versus Colombia."

"I thought the women play Colombia."

Brian snorts. "The nation has a men's team, too, you know. Anyway, you're up, Wesley. I already emailed you the info. Best get yourself to the airport."

Brian hangs up and I stare at my phone in disbelief. Did I really just get called up to play for my country? I swallow, a thick knot of … something … sticking in my throat.

Cara rolls over and squints at me through sleepy eyes. "What was that about?" She rubs at her face.

"Shh. Don't get up."

She sits up. "I want to know what the call was about. You can tell me shit, too, Wes. I'm not totally fixated on my own problems."

"Hey, that wasn't what I was doing. I know you've got room for more than one thought at a time." I grin at her and kiss her cheek. She arches a brow and gestures for me to go on. I take a deep breath. "I got invited to the national team camp."

Her eyes fly wide. "Wes. That's amazing!" She takes a breath. Her face falls. "Oh."

"Yeah. Oh." I lean against her headboard, elbows on my knees and face in my hands.

Neither of us says anything, waiting for the other to speak. My mouth is dry and it's like someone poured sand on my tongue.

"What do you want me to say here?"

"I don't know. This has been my whole life. My only dream."

"I know that. And I know you know it's my dream, too."

I nod. "This is how we met in the first place—both of us chasing this goal. And now it's here at my fingertips."

She nods. She clenches her teeth. I think about how this chance might not come again. She just stares at me. I sputter. "You saw how an injury took me out this year. You saw that."

"What are you saying?" I tug on my hair, considering my words, but she spits out, "It should be an automatic no. No discussion."

"What the fuck?" Is she seriously dictating the terms of my career to me here? "Are you my dad now? Telling me what's best? This isn't just some snap decision I can push away without considering options."

Cara closes her eyes. Her chest expands as she takes a deep breath and then lets it out slowly. "I think you should go."

"I didn't say that."

"No, I mean I think you should leave my apartment. Right now, please."

"Cara, wait. We have to talk through this."

She shakes her head and points to the door. My phone rings again, Brian's piercing ringtone, insistent. "I have to take this."

"I said get out." Her tone leaves no room for discussion, so I grab my shoes and leave, the pinging shrieks from my phone chasing me down the hall like the horns of Jericho.

CHAPTER 30
CARA

I HEAR voices coming from my living room. I must have fallen asleep after I kicked Wes out of my room, because the light has shifted and it's nearly dark outside. I figure Jay must have invited people over, and I am about to pull a pillow over my head to ignore them when one of the voices floats close to my door. It's familiar.

"Cara, chica, get your cute behind out here." A series of knocks shake my door as the sleep fog dissipates.

"Rosalie?" I climb out of bed and shuffle to the door, opening it to see not only Rose, but Shante and Toni as well. My mouth drops open. Jay stands behind them, grinning.

My Midfield Mamis swarm into me, tackling me into the wall and squeezing me, muttering praise in Cuban and Puerto Rican slang as we all jump up and down.

"How are you here?" I pull my head out of the bramble of curls and hugging hands.

Shante pats my face. "We were going to come to your game against Colombia anyway." She shrugs. "Jay helped us switch our travel plans."

I clutch at my heart. "Is it possible to die of happiness? I'm so glad you guys are all here."

Toni shakes a finger at me. "You are not allowed to die, querida. Not with those feet."

Within ten minutes, I'm hustled to the sofa with my feet in a pan of warm water, the familiar sounds and smells of my former roommates surrounding me as I watch them initiate my current roommate into the healing wonders of a soothing pedicure.

"You owe me for this, Moreno," Jay says, but I can tell she's enjoying the feel of the warm water on her tired feet.

Shante has a laptop open, curating headlines and telling me there's something she wants me to see. "There's a hashtag. Did you know about the hashtag?"

I nod. "Yeah. I like it. We stand with Cara." I can't hold back my smile at the thought of that, even if it is only a few people among a loud chorus of assholes using different hashtags about the situation.

"No." Shante shakes her head. "No, I mean it's a trending hashtag, Cara. Look." She spins the screen so I can see. "There are over ten million posts from women supporting you, around the world."

My eyes adjust to the screen, and I see the posts, more each second. Stories of harassment at work and feeling inspired to speak up. Girls in high school posting about talking to the school board about equal equipment and field access. And dozens and dozens of former national team players who have experienced unwanted touches from Lou Rubeo.

"Oh my god." I point at the screen. "This is…"

"A tidal wave." Toni pulls my foot out of the water and up onto her lap and starts hacking at my heels with a pumice stone. "You threw a pebble into the ocean, and the ripples made a fucking tsunami."

With a triumphant huff, Shante pulls up a video. It's a compilation from the current national team. Everyone apparently sent in videos from their own homes, explaining the boycott and how they're not going to stand for this treatment from our national office.

"This is more than I ever thought I wanted," I whisper.

My friends squeeze me in support. "All eyes are on you," Rosalie chirps. "We see you. The world sees you. You have everything now."

A sob roars from my chest. "But I don't have Wes. He didn't stay."

Jay growls as I explain what happened before they turned up at the apartment. "Get me a hunting permit, Rosalie. I'm going to shoot a Stag."

"Fuck this guy. He had his chance." Shante slams the laptop shut. "We've got other shit to worry about." She holds out a selection of nail polish for me. "I'm thinking red. For the blood of your enemies."

"Where are my enemies? I mean, currently."

"We're doing a press conference, roomie." Jay smiles and pulls a piece of paper from her pocket. "In a few hours we're meeting at the stadium with Alex Steele, Lucy, all those folks. You get to read our statement out loud."

"Our statement?"

Jay grins and explains that our series of emails and text messages with the national team is now assembled as a manifesto, a set of demands for the international sporting body to clean house in the national office or risk the US women not participating in the Paris Olympics. The team manager even put together a list of financial hits the program will take without our national team out there driving ticket sales, merchandise sales, and premium television viewers.

"We're going to rain on them like molten, hot metal until they slice that misogynist cancer from the office." Toni nods definitively. "Now let's get you dressed."

CHAPTER 31
WES

I DON'T EVEN LOOK at what I'm packing in my bag back at my apartment. I don't remember the drive over here, either. I keep seeing Cara's face, so hurt and angry, and then I remember my own face when my uncle took me and my cousins to watch the national team play for the first time.

I was five years old with my face pressed against the bleacher railing, staring at the guys on the field, desperate to be among them someday. And even though I fought like hell through my injuries, I don't know if I truly believed I'd be here, invited to put on the Stars and Stripes to represent my country on the soccer field.

Like, who turns down this kind of opportunity?

Cara does. For good reason.

I don't know how to silence the voice in my head telling me I'm making the wrong choice. This has been my only choice for as long as I remember. I grab my cleats and shove them in my duffle bag. My flight leaves in three hours. I don't have time for second thoughts.

But my guts are roiling and I search for my phone. I can take a few minutes to call Uncle Hawk and ask him what to do. He's no stranger to this opportunity and he knows the stakes. I press the icon for his contact, waiting for the call to connect.

And I realize he's probably at home with Aunt Lucy, comforting her because *she* isn't with the national team right now, either. A wave of shame rolls over me, thinking about her getting fired and all the power of my family backing her up didn't change a goddamned thing.

I hang up the phone before Uncle Hawk can answer.

I stare out my window, even though it's dark and I can't see outside. I know what's out there: an entire world divided into people who are sick of the shit Cara and all women have to endure...and scumbags who let it continue by turning the other way.

"Fuck!" I scream and bury my hands in my hair, hoping I can somehow tug it all out in one symbolic yank.

I call Cara and she sends my call right to voicemail, but I deserve that. I wait for the robotic voice to finish and I blurt, "Cara. I'm passing up my chance. I'm taking a stand with you." And then, because it's true and overwhelming and necessary, I add, "I love you. I'm coming to find you and tell you in person."

CHAPTER 32
CARA

COACH LUCY, Jay and I take our seats at the table in the press room, which is currently empty because the stadium staff is giving us a minute to get our bearings before unleashing the hounds. And I know they're hungry as actual feral dogs for the scoop on this situation, especially as the men's team gathers in California for their international friendly match.

The thought of the men's team turns my stomach sour and I worry I might puke until Jay squeezes my hand on the table. I nod and Coach Lucy waves a hand at the guard at the door. He opens the swinging metal panel and a herd of cameras, microphones, and hairspray shuffles past him.

The seats in the room fill immediately and interns rush to bring microphones to the table, flashbulbs popping as photographers adjust their settings for the lighting in the room. I tune it all out and think about the statement I'm about to read.

Coach Lucy taps on the microphone a few times and the din settles down. "Thank you for being here tonight," she says. "I'm Lucy Moyer, former assistant coach for the women's national soccer team."

The press erupts into angry shouts and Lucy holds up a hand. "I say former because, as I'm sure you know by now, I was dismissed from my position after expressing my concern that one of my players was being harassed by the president of our national organization." Lucy purses her lips and I clench my butt, knowing it's almost my turn to talk to the cameras. "Rather than examine the issue, the national office sent me home hours before the team played an international match. And I think you all know what happened after that."

Another roar from the press. Hands wave in the air and everyone speaks on top of one another. The sound throbs through the room, the bright lights pulsing. I can't see or think. My phone starts ringing in my pocket and I smash the button to send the call to voicemail.

Lucy holds up her hand again and stands, pulling the microphone up with her. "At this time, Cara Moreno will read a statement from the collective players from the national team, about their choice to boycott this weekend's camp and match. Cara?"

Mercifully, the crowd of reporters remains quiet as I clear my throat and adjust the paper. "Thanks. Um, thank you all for being here." I glance up at them and they all stare. "I'm not used to the spotlight like this. I never wanted to be up here making statements." I clear my throat again, more aggressively, and Jay slides me a cup of water, which I clutch in one hand. "I just want to play soccer. All of us on the national team … we just want to play soccer. We aren't out here to be pretty. We aren't looking for relationships. We just want to play the game."

I pause to sip the water and hope the press will hold off their flood of questions until I read the whole statement. "Those of us playing professionally, we do so with lower salaries than our male counterparts, even if we score more goals and win more games. But we aren't here talking about that injustice." I stare at the crowd again. They wait, but I do see red lights flashing from the cameras, so I know this is being broadcast live ... everywhere. "We are here, back at our homes and not in California, because our governing body is being led by a predator. A man who grabs women against our consent and kisses us without permission, who corners us in hallways to talk about our bodies...this is not a man who views us as professional colleagues. This is predatory behavior that has no home in any workplace. Because that's what professional soccer is for us: our work. This is our career. We train and we study, and we fight for this nation, for this sport, as professionals, and we demand to be treated as such."

I take a giant breath and see Jay nodding out of the corner of my eye. "That is why none of the women named to the national team squad will agree to play for this country until Lou Rubeo is removed from his position, and until the board that refused to discipline him is removed from their seats." I look over at Coach Lucy, who pumps her fist at me quietly. I nod. "We will now take your questions."

Another thunderstorm of noise erupts from the crowd, and I've never navigated one of these situations before, so I sit back in my chair and wait for someone to tell me what to do. Lucy is more adept at this atmosphere, and she points at a woman in the front row. "Pam. Go ahead."

The woman stands up. I gasp when I see she's wearing a shirt that says #WeStandWithCara. She smiles at me. "Pam O'Reilly. Fem Forward Press. Cara, what does it feel like to speak up after this abuse, and inspire so many other women to do the same?"

"Pardon?"

Pam smiles wider. "Our last count showed over 15,000 testimonials online of women and people of other marginalized genders who have spoken out against harassment or abuse in the workplace since hearing your story. Can you comment on how it feels to lead that movement?"

I blink at her a few times. "I didn't want to lead a movement. I just want to play soccer. I want everyone to be able to do what they want to do without worrying about anyone crossing a line."

Pam scribbles on her notepad, smiles, and sits. Lucy points to someone else in the crowd, who directs their question right back at her, so I take a few moments to catch my breath. I glance at my phone and see there's a voicemail from Wes. I start sweating because he's supposed to be on a flight into enemy territory right now. But I'll have to deal with that later. In my periphery, I see movement at the side of the table and notice some murmurs, but I keep my eye on the crowd, surprised to find more faces that seem supportive than the angry macho crowd I feared.

Lucy points to a guy near the back of the room, who stands and introduces himself as Peter Winters from Sports Daily News. "Yes, Cara, can you comment on why nobody from the men's national team seems to have a problem with Lou Rubeo or his leadership? Seems like if he was such a bad president, there would be unrest from that camp as well?"

I open my mouth to tell Peter that the men aren't experiencing sexism from Rubeo, when someone interrupts me. "One small correction there for you, Pete."

I turn my head to see Wes standing by the table, wearing a US jersey from a few decades ago. I furrow my brow and Wes smiles at me hopefully. Peter gives Wes a "go on" gesture to see what sort of correction Wes might have for him.

Wes reaches for the microphone, which I hand him. "There *is* unrest with the men's national team. I, Wesley Stag, was recently named left wing for the squad and am joining the women's team in their boycott. Anyone who grabs a woman and kisses her without consent has no business leading an organization. The game and this nation mean too much to me to agree to play under conditions like that." Wes peels off his jersey and throws it on the table. "I stand with Cara and the national team, demanding that Rubeo be fired, and the board replaced." Wes crosses his arms over his chest and indeed remains standing.

A tear slides down my cheek and relief washes over me. A ragged sob escapes my mouth and I press my hand over my lips to avoid it getting picked up by the microphones.

Lucy and Jay handle questions for I don't know how long and eventually the security guard ushers the press from the room. Finally, the only people left are Lucy, Jay, and Wes standing around me.

Lucy dips in to squeeze me in a hug. "Cara, you were fantastic. Total class act." I see her look up at Wes and smile. She rests a hand on his shoulder. "Good to see you, nephew."

"Thanks. I'm just glad I made it in time." They grin at each other until Jay groans and stands up.

"All right, all right." She claps her hands. "Who is taking me for pasta? I haven't had wheat in like five months, and I think this warrants a good emotional eat."

Coach Lucy smiles. "I'll take you up on that. Mind if we call my husband on the way?"

"I'm here, babe." Hawk Moyer pokes his head in the door, grinning. "Proud of you all." He blows his wife a kiss and Lucy and Jay make their way over to him, leaving me alone in the room with Wes and his balled up national team jersey.

Wes slides his hands into the pockets of his sweatpants and looks down at me. "My agent is pretty pissed I didn't tell him I was skipping my flight."

"Oh yeah?"

He nods. "He'll get over it." I tap at the table and Wes slides into the folding chair at my side. "I couldn't go through with it, Cara. I'm sorry I wasn't strong enough to say no right away. You deserve someone who stands by your side no matter what."

I press my lips together and try not to cry.

Wes reaches for my chin, and I tilt my head into his palm.

His voice is a whisper as he says, "I want you to know how much I admire your strength. How much my entire family supports you as a player. God, Cara, you are like fire on that field and all I want in the world is to see you back out there."

"All you want? Really?"

He grins. "I mean, I'd take another date with you as an add-on. But yeah, babe. I want you to do what you were born to do." He fishes in his pocket and pulls out his phone. "Here," he says. "Look." Wes slides the phone across the table to me so I can see a photo of him standing with his arms raise, the dark hairs of his lower belly visible beneath the hem of his T-shirt as he screams in unadulterated joy. I can see a room packed with people in similar poses. "That's when you scored your third goal against Jamaica. That's my entire family watching you, so proud of what you can do."

I clutch the phone to my chest, swelling with emotions I don't know how to name. I've never had an extended family watch my game, let alone cheer for me in unison. Wes reaches for my face with his other hand, and I drop the phone, moving my hands to rest on his thighs as he stares into my eyes. "Cara, you make me a better player, but more important, you make me want to be a better man. You are the piece I've been missing my whole life." He draws a shaky inhale. "I need you, Cara. I love you."

I open my mouth to say I love him, too, that I need him and his big, noisy family that will hopefully continue to butt in when either of us loses our way momentarily. But Tim Stag bursts into the room with my lawyer, Tawnya, at his heels. "We have news, kids."

We whip our heads over to stare at the intruders. Tim smiles. "Rubeo. Is. Out."

CHAPTER 33
CARA

WES ASKS if he can drive me home after our late dinner at the restaurant. Considering I drove down here crammed in the back seat of Jay's sedan with Shante and Rosalie, with Toni up front admiring all the Pittsburgh lights on the water, I was more than happy to accept a more spacious ride.

Once we're in the car, alone, Wes turns to face me before putting his key in the ignition. "Cara, I know I have a lot of atoning to do. A long way to go to prove that I'm solid, but —"

I place a finger over his lips and lean across the console to kiss him. I tug on his shirt, pulling him closer, savoring the taste of him. It's been days since we've been physically intimate. Weeks maybe? I've lost track of time with everything that's been happening in my life. "I need you," I whisper against his lips, and the responding moan from his chest tells me all I need to know about his state of mind.

He swallows, and turns the engine over, and I settle into my seat facing him as best I can. "I thought you'd be shirtless when you pulled that jersey off." I reach across the gear shift for his leg, tracing along the muscle with my index finger.

"You wish." I can see his grin in the light from the street lamps along the bridge as he heads toward my place. "That would have been an entirely different sort of statement if I hadn't had an undershirt on…"

I hum contentedly along with the music, enjoying the look of him as we make our way to my apartment. "I have four women camping in my apartment right now," I mutter, realizing this is the first time I've seen my friends in person in months.

"I don't mind. They're important to you." Wes shrugs. "You're important to me."

A smile tugs at my lips and I remember something I wanted to tell him earlier, before things got heated. "I called you my boyfriend. A couple times. Is that okay?"

Wes turns to look at me, slaps the turn signal, and pulls to the side of the road. "Cara." He punches the button for his four-way flashers. "You can call me whatever the hell you want. I've been yours from the moment I laid eyes on you. I fucking love you, remember?"

Something warm spreads through me and I do remember. I remember that I was about to say it back to him before his uncle burst in the room with legal updates about our case. Both the men's and women's national team camps have been rescheduled, and Wes and I fly to California together in a few days, along with Jay and Lucy. Both the Forge and Hot Metal have plans for an airport sendoff for us that, frankly, sounds more exciting than any team-sponsored celebration we've had yet in the Steel City.

"I remember something like that." I squeeze his leg. "I'm bad at this kind of thing."

"What? Being a rock star?" Wes tucks my hair behind my ear, his elbows bumping against all the different knobs and gadgets in a car that's too small for his long limbs.

I grin into his hand as he strokes a thumb across my lip.

"I'm bad at verbalizing my feelings. I'm used to expressing myself physically."

Wes's teeth shine white as he grins at me under the street-lamp. "I'm happy to have that sort of conversation with you, Cara Moreno."

"Good. Take me home, Stag."

————

We arrive at my apartment to a flurry of activity. I see Jay in the middle of a circle of my friends, who are applying hair pomade and glitter with gusto. "Jay …" I clutch at the door frame for support. "Are you wearing makeup?"

She bats her lashes at me and flexes, looking cute as hell in a shirt, tie and fitted pants. My chicas are in heels and skirts with gold hoops and popping curls. Toni smacks her hands together and turns to face me. "Jay's taking us to a gay bar. You aren't invited, pana."

"You're not taking me out with you?"

Rosalie points at me. "You seem tired … or at least like you want to be in bed." She smooths her down her shirt. "This pansexual princess is looking to dance," she says, twirling.

Shante and Toni bust out laughing and Jay pulls her phone from her pants pocket. "Ladies, our ride is outside." She winks at me. "We'll be gone for hours."

And just like that, they're off in a cloud of expensive perfume and laughter. Wes wastes no time closing the door behind them and locking it, then backing me up against the kitchen island. "Do you want to dance, Cara? I'm very good with feet."

I swat at his chest. "I don't think you meant that how it sounds."

He arches a brow at me. "How did it sound?"

Biting a lip, I rock back and drink him in. I can see the lines of his abs through the undershirt, the bulge in his pants that pulses along with his breath. "It sounded like you're going to suck on my toes again."

Wes growls and hauls me over his shoulder, his steps eating the distance between the kitchen and my bedroom. He kicks the door shut behind him and tosses me on the mattress. I clear my hair from my face and gaze up at him, the adrenaline from this evening settling in my stomach. Or is that arousal?

It all comes out to the same thing as I gaze up at the look on his face. Wesley Stag has sex seeping from his pores, from the dark stubble on his chin to the blown pupils in his gray eyes, to the hot cock pressing against my belly as he holds himself above my body, staring. "I love you, Cara."

My face melts into a smile and I adjust myself, taking more of his weight onto my groin, where the friction feels perfect. "I love you, too, Wes. And I want you. Real bad."

His mouth hooks to the side in a crooked smile. "Anything you want." Pivoting to the side and freeing up his arms, Wes reaches behind his neck to pull off his undershirt with one arm. I wriggle out of my top and pull down my pants, reaching for my bra to remove it until he stops me with a gentle hand.

"Can I?" I nod and he pulls the straps down from my shoulders. I usually wear sports bras. I'm not even sure if Wes has ever seen me in a regular bra and panties, but he seems super interested in the sight at the moment. He rocks back to sit on his heels, staring at me as he traces his hands along my side, fingers grazing the cotton at my hips, the cups of my bra.

"My god, Cara, you're everything I've ever wanted. Look at you." I glance down, seeing myself through his eyes. And I smile at the sight of his lips on my skin. I love the contrast between our skin tones. I love the feel of his big hands across my belly. And I love the sounds he makes as he pinches my nipples before licking each of them thoroughly.

Somehow, we both wind up naked and curled together, kissing and sucking each other's skin until I'm worried we'll both be covered in hickies. Wes seems less concerned, asking for more when I latch on to his neck right where it meets his shoulder. I suck harder and he groans, pressing his hips into mine so powerfully I nearly come from the contact.

My gasp brings him back into the moment and he draws back, adjusting his position again so he can fit a hand between my legs. "I want you to come first, because I'm not going to last."

I shake my head. "I want you inside me. Please, Wes? Oh, god, that feels so good."

He bites his lip, pressing his thumb against my clit and meeting my eye, seeking permission to keep going on his quest to get me off. "Fine. Okay. Oh, yes. Like that. Wow." I sit up on my forearms, watching as Wes moves his hand in my wetness. I watch as his fingers disappear inside my body, surrounded by sensation as his touch seems to spread through my entire nervous system.

"You're so damn beautiful when you come for me. I love making you feel good." He rocks his hips against my thigh, like he can't bear to not be moving, and I reach for him greedily, clenching my fist around his length. We taste each other's moans as I kiss him while he rubs until I soar over the edge, coming in his arms, knowing this is the man who would give up everything he's ever dreamed of for the chance to support me, to do what's right.

I'm still coming when Wes slips inside me, and I open my eyes to find his face an inch from mine. I am filled with him, stretched magnificently around his hot, smooth cock, and I feel closer to him than ever before. "I love you," I whimper as I start to move beneath him. "I love you so much."

"Cara. Fuck, baby. I have to come. You feel so good, and I

love you so damn much." Wes thrusts a few more times and I feel the muscles of his butt work as he moves. And then he stiffens, and I feel his release, over and over, warm and pulsing. But more than that I feel the tears on his cheeks as he rests his face against mine, telling me over and over how much he needs me, how he will never, ever let me go.

CHAPTER 34
WES

"YO, Cara, Jay, you guys ready to go?" Wyatt, impatient as always, hollers down the hall to my girl and her roommate. We have hours until the three of us fly with Aunt Lucy to play rescheduled matches with the national teams, but Wyatt insists we go early. He doesn't want to stick around the airport for the press circus, mumbling something about keeping a low profile.

Me? I can't wait for the attention as the four of us head out to meet the new Soccer USA president Eloise Lisange, who immediately reinstated Aunt Lucy to the women's team coaching staff and gave her and Akemi a giant pay raise.

"Coming!" Cara staggers out of her bedroom under the weight of two duffel bags. She will be out in Cali for a bit after the match because her agent landed her some pretty slick endorsement deals and she'll be shooting commercials. Both of us made arrangements to keep up our therapy sessions remotely while we're traveling with the national team, and I've been surprised by how much I'm learning in those conversations.

I rush forward to take one of the bags from Cara, but she

shakes her head. "I got it, babe. Save your back for the match against Colombia."

I wink at her. "I'll save my back for you, baby, and lie on it gladly."

"Gross. I'm going to turn on the car." Wyatt huffs out of the apartment with Cara on his heels, the clips on her bag squeaking as she walks.

I hear her phone chirp, and she pauses to check it, mouthing that it's her mom on the line. "Mama? Papi? Yes, I'm on my way to the airport right now." She smiles. Things have improved ever so slightly with her parents since Cara gave that press conference on television and Telemundo did a feature piece on her as America's "it" sports star. Cara's voice fades as she makes her way down the stairs with Wyatt, but she sounds happy telling her parents about the game schedule.

My stuff is already loaded in Uncle Ty's minivan, so I poke my head in Jay's room to see if she needs any help.

I catch a glimpse of her rainbow stack of keeper jerseys as she zips her bag shut with a flourish. "Had to get the lucky socks squeezed in the corners, but I fit everything in one bag."

"Nicely done." I glance around to see if she actually only has the one bag. "Need a hand with anything?"

She clips a belt bag around her waist and slaps me on the shoulder. "I'm good, Stagly. Looking forward to a few nights without you sleeping down the hall."

She steps through the door, and I follow her so she can lock up. I lean on the wall and tell her, "I've been trying to get Cara to stay at my place to give you privacy."

"Oh, sure, it's *me* who needs privacy." Jay rolls her eyes and heads for the stairwell. I can hear the bass thumping in the minivan from the lobby of the building and I have to laugh at the tricked-out sound system in a Honda Odyssey with 200,000 miles on it.

Wyatt barely waits for the sliding doors to close before he

stomps on the gas. Jay turns around from the front seat and shakes her head at me when she sees that I've reached across the aisle between the captains chairs to hold Cara's hand. "What?"

"I'm going to miss you, Moreno."

Cara furrows her brow. "What do you mean?" I squeeze her hand tighter while we wait for Jay to elaborate.

Wyatt grunts. "She means you're going to have to start staying at Wesley's solo pad, so you don't keep her up at night with your sex-capades."

Cara's cheeks flush but I refuse to feel embarrassed about the sounds I can draw from my girlfriend when I'm doling out multiple o's. And I'm overjoyed at the idea of her spending more time at my place, just the two of us. I pull her hand closer to me and lean over so I can kiss her knuckles.

We pull in front of the domestic terminal at the airport, and I see Wyatt clench his jaw. He hates the press and I know he wants to get out of here before anyone notices us as part of the celebratory send-off. I hop out and pull our bags from the back of the van and barely get my head out of the way as he closes the door via a button by the steering wheel. "Play hard, guys. Go USA!" He zooms away before we can respond.

Cara and Jay are grinning as they head toward the sliding doors to the bag drop. Both our teams fill the landside terminal, along with fans of the Iron Army ... and all their drums, cowbells, and giant black-and-yellow flags. Cara starts dancing to the beat of the drum line as we walk in with our bags and the Hot Metal women notice our arrival.

"They're here," someone shouts into a megaphone. And all hell breaks loose as forty pro soccer players, our coaches, and our most rabid fans start chanting "I believe that we will win." Jay drops her bag and starts clapping along with the beat and Cara follows suit. I have no choice but to drop my own bag and twirl my best girl, dipping her for a kiss to the roar of the crowd.

Someone shows up with a tuba and only then does airport security intervene and try to shuffle us to the security line. But Cara, Jay and I all have pre-check, so we make our way to Aunt Lucy, who has a microphone and speaker that one of the fans must have set up for her. "Thank you, Pittsburgh, for this incredible send off."

The crowd roars. People pause on their way to their flights, taking pictures and cheering "USA, USA" before they head into the security line. This right here is how I always knew it would feel to reach this level of competition.

But I never dared to imagine I'd be here alongside a woman playing at this same level, that I could focus as much on her as I do my career—more intently, actually—and instead of turning my dreams to dust my relationship would fill me with more joy than a game-winning goal.

"Cara, Jay and I cannot wait to show you what a united national team can do under great leadership." I hear Aunt Lucy's voice and I pull myself together by pulling Cara tight against my side. She rests her head on my shoulder and hugs my arm. Lucy points at me and I wave at the crowd. "And my nephew, Wesley Stag, is excited to kick in a new era of men's soccer on a team committed to building equity at all levels of the game. Right Wes?"

"Absolutely." My words are drowned by another roar of the crowd. We wave and sign a few autographs before Jay starts tapping at her watch and the four of us make our way through the security line. I recognize the security agent who held me up for a pat-down the first time I flew to California for one of these camps. I give him a salute as he glances over my shoulder at the crowd, still pressing right up against the barricade to cheer us off.

I smile at Cara as I reach for our bags. She yanks hers from my hand and wags a finger at me and tips her head toward the shuttle to our gate. I press into the train car, snuggling up against her as if the car is overflowing when really, it's mostly empty. Cara laughs and leans in to my embrace. "I love you, Wes. I can't imagine being here without you."

I run a hand through her hair and kiss the top of her head. "I love you, too, Cara. And you're never going to be without me again."

EPILOGUE: WES
THE PARIS OLYMPICS

THE US MEN'S team got knocked out in the first round, but that's pretty much what everyone expected. I didn't mind because it freed up all my time to watch Cara play, watch Cara take press interviews, and watch her sponsors shower her with gifts and good-luck flowers.

My girl is starting to get comfortable in the spotlight, but she still flushes the most beautiful shade of rose when people say something particularly complimentary about her athletic prowess.

Today was the semifinal match against Sweden and I was right there in the front row with Cara's college roommates when she scored the game winning goal. Honestly, I think I strained my back a little bit cheering as my lady whipped off her jersey and took a victory lap, abs flexing like a bad-ass. Cara's parents even texted me that they were impressed, and I promised to pass their felicidades along to her.

But first, my girlfriend needs post-match recovery, and I have big plans to take care of her. I've been extremely patient, helping little kids in line for her autograph and taking pictures, texting the Stag family back home with all the important updates like yes, Cara

received Aunt Alice's care package and yes, she's definitely still moving in with me once we get back to
Pittsburgh.

I made arrangements with Aunt Lucy for Cara to take her
ice bath separate from the rest of the team. After she signs the
final autograph and waves at the fans, Cara says, "Sorry,
guys. I have to do my cool down so I'm ready for Australia in
the final in a few days."

I put two fingers in my mouth and whistle, kicking off a
new wave of "USA, USA" chants as Cara makes her way to
the locker room. I know what she will find there: instructions
for her post-game recovery session in a different location than
she's expecting. I'm waiting in the hydro therapy room with
fluffy towels and massage oil when Cara sticks her face in the
door.

"Wes?" Her brow is furrowed in confusion. "Where's the
rest of the team?"

I shrug. "I didn't check their recovery schedule, baby.
Only yours."

She crosses her arms over her chest, and I can see her
wiggling her toes, painted bright red this time, apparently for
the blood of her on-field rivals ... according to Rosalie. "Does
Coach Lucy know you're in here with me?"

"Babe." I set the towels on the bench next to the small pool
of icy water. "Someone has to time you and make sure you
don't stay in there too long. I don't want you to get
hypothermia."

Cara laughs and kicks off her sandals, sliding her shorts
down to reveal the hottest little pair of booty shorts. I hope
she plans to take them off for her ice bath, but I'm out of luck
in that regard as she starts to slither into the water in her
sports bra and those perfect underwear.

I lick my lips as she hisses, sinking up to her armpits and
resting her head on the side of the pool. "I should tug you in
here with me."

"Nah." I squat down beside her. "I didn't play today. And my body heat would warm up the water too much."

Cara's teeth start chattering and I see huge goose bumps on her lovely, coppery skin. I glance at my watch. "Nine minutes left." She growls. "I know it sucks. But you're going to sleep so well tonight."

She splashes me and damn. That water is frigid. But I fully intend to warm her up after she's done in there, so I don't worry too much about my damp shirt. We have this room to ourselves and there's a perfectly lovely cushioned bench along the back wall.

"Take my mind off of this. Tell me what you thought of the game."

"Damn, baby. It was outstanding." We piece the match together verbally and I love the expression on her face as she describes sending that final kick right past that Swedish keeper's fingertips. "I didn't think anyone would get past her this tournament. Didn't she have a perfect save record before now?"

Cara smiles contentedly, her arms stiff against the sides of the cold pool. My watch alarm beeps, and she springs from the water like she was launched out by a rocket. I barely get to my feet in time to open the towel and grab her. "Why do we do this to ourselves?"

I shake my head as I rub her through the towel, trying to warm her arms. "They say it helps our central nervous systems. Or the lactic acid. Or something."

"Something." She rests her wet head on my shoulder, and I guide us both toward the bench, easing her until she's lying down, big brown eyes fixed on mine. "What are you going to do now?"

I grin. "Now I'm going to warm you up." I pull the bottle of massage oil from my pocket and wave it at her, enjoying the sleepy, contented expression on her face as I squirt some of the oil into my hand. "Why don't you take off those wet clothes?"

"Too tired." She curls the towel more tightly around herself and I reach for a foot, massaging the arch the way I know she loves, drawing beautiful groans from her mouth, that melt into moans when I chase my touch with kisses.

"Do you want me to help you take them off?" She nods her head. "Let's just start with the bottoms and see how that feels, okay?" I love acting like this is some sort of clinical examination instead of me preparing to fuck her senseless and then carry her up to her room to tuck her into bed by curfew. Cara lifts her hips and I slide the wet undies off. I shove them into my pocket, despite being soaking wet, because I plan to use them later when I'm alone in my own room.

I slick up my hands with more of the oil and work my palms along her legs, massaging her calves and firm thighs as she spreads her legs wider, resting her feet on the floor on either side of the bench. "That's it, Cara. Perfect."

I lean in a nose her mound as she opens wider before I slide a slicked-up finger into her folds, parting her for me as Cara's chest rises and falls more rapidly. "That feels so good."

"Mm, it's all for you, baby. Is that enough pressure?" I study her face for a beat and add another finger inside her, resulting in a huge buck of her hips and her hands slapping down on my shoulders. "All right. Maybe just one more finger, then?" When I slide the third finger into her heat, Cara keens, raising up onto her elbows with her mouth in a tight oh. She breathes through her nose, and I can tell she's trying to keep things quiet. "Don't worry. I locked the door."

Cara nods and lies back on the bench as I fuck her slowly with my hand. Once I feel the pulsing flutters inside her, I know she's close. I lean forward and lick her, tasting salt and musk and perfection as she whimpers my name. I love the sound of my name on her lips. *My* name. And I'm so turned on by her pleasure that I almost come in my track pants.

"Wes, please." She eases up onto her forearms again, staring at me.

"Please what, Cara?" I slide my hand out of her body one finger at a time. I know what she wants, but I want to hear her say it.

"Please fuck me. I need your cock."

I promised her I'd never leave her wanting, ever again. So, I quickly shove my pants down below my butt and pull out my dick, which is so hard it bobs against my stomach as I position myself between Cara's legs. My eyes latch onto hers as I slide home and I feel her body relax, like this was exactly what she needed to totally let go.

Cara reaches for my waist as I bring my hands to either side of her head. My body is bent at an awkward angle, but I don't care about anything except this connection we share. "I love you, Cara. Always." I grunt, driving into her as she starts to come. She moves to hold a hand over her mouth to muffle her cries, but I kiss her instead, swallowing her moans and feeding her mine in exchange.

I feel her orgasm rip through her and mine is close behind, starting at the base of my spine and tearing through my body as I mutter into her ear over and over. "I love you. I need you. You are incredible."

After I get Cara bundled up in cozy sweats, I user her outside to where I booked a car service. She doesn't have another match for a few days, and her coaches said there are no team meetings this evening. She's all mine at the Olympic Village … until curfew, of course.

Cara leans a sleepy head on my shoulder, humming contentedly along with the radio, and we hold hands as we walk to her room. I'm prepared for anything, whatever she needs, but I'm really hoping she wants me here with her. When Cara opens the door to her room, I'm glad to see housekeeping has delivered the care package of food from Aunt Alice. Both our stomachs growl audibly when we're hit with the aroma of freshly-cooked food.

Cara darts into the room and opens the box, moaning out an "mmm" that goes straight to my groin. I'm about to slip out the door and let her eat, when she calls for me. "Will you eat with me?"

"Of course. Not even a question." I close the door and walk toward the table and chairs. Cara sits and rests her chin on one hand, reaching for me with the other. "Will you stay until I fall asleep?"

A wave of warmth floods over me and I scoot my chair closer to hers, so her body touches mine while we eat until we're stuffed. Cara gets ready for bed while I clean up, and then we climb into bed together.

I rub her arm as she drifts off and I fight hard to stay awake. My thoughts wander to the future, to a lifetime of us supporting each other on the field and strengthening our connection off of it.

Once her breathing slows and I know she's asleep, I press a kiss to her temple and slide out of her room. I rest my head against the door, hating the national team rules that keep us separated right now but honoring her commitment to following them.

My phone buzzes as I head to my own room and I see a text from Wyatt. I click it open, expecting some sort of celebration after the women's game today. Instead, it's a series of angry emojis followed by a chilling line of text.

> I don't know what to do, cuz. My bio dad showed up today.

————

Thank you so much for reading Wes and Cara's story! Wyatt's book, Forging Legacy, is coming soon.

Want one more glimpse of Wes and Cara's happily ever after? My newsletter subscribers get a spicy bonus scene. Visit laineydavis.com to sign up for a post-workout workout story.

Have you met Wes's parents, Thatcher and Emma? Find their happily ever after in Fragile Illusion.

AUTHOR'S NOTE

I had the incredible fortune to travel to New Zealand and Australia for the 2023 Women's Football World Cup. I sat with 75,000 people in Stadium Australia, cheering for women. I had never experienced anything like it—the atmosphere was absolutely exhilarating. We traveled home after the round of 16 and watched the rest of the matches on television, waking at 4 in the morning to catch them live.

As the final match ended, I noticed there was a man on the stage who seemed overly familiar with the Spanish champions. And then he picked one of them up. And then … he kissed her. On the mouth.

I remember asking my husband if he noticed, and of course he had. The camera later showed the same man grabbing his crotch in "celebration" when Spain won.

I couldn't get it out of my head.

The incident haunted me with such visceral anger that I put my book production schedule on hold so I could work through my feelings with fiction.

I began to imagine a character at the top of her game, just trying to play some damn soccer, and what might happen if a man in power did the same thing to my fictional heroine.

I actually began writing the book as the incident exploded throughout international media. Women around the world wrote statements of support for the Spanish athletes. News outlets portrayed the whole thing as either an outrage or a gross overreaction. The perpetrator's mother went on a hunger strike in protest of his good name being dragged through the mud while his other relatives told stories of similar acts of harassment. Every day, I texted my author fried Liz Lincoln that the story was writing itself.

My story, Forging Glory, is fictional. But these sorts of things happen every day. Over and over.

I owe a debt of gratitude to all the women and people of marginalized genders who have stood up to the people in power looking to objectify, harass, and otherwise abuse their position.

As for the book, I offer many thanks to Liz Alden, Elise Kennedy, Melissa Wiesner, Nicky Lewis and Elizabeth Perry for input on my drafts.

I tried to write Cara authentically and I relied on Cuban American readers and their lived experiences to support the creation of Cara and her friends. In particular, Victoria Saccenti and Shawn Alfonso Wells helped me to shape my characters, their dialogue, and their interactions.

I'm grateful to Felicia Perez for her administrative and marking support and I thank Becky with Bookcase Media for her keen editorial eye.

ALSO BY LAINEY DAVIS

Bridges and Bitters series

Fireball: An Enemies to Lovers Romance (Sam and AJ)

Liquid Courage: A Marriage in Crisis Romance (Chloe and Teddy)

Speed Rail: A Single Dad Romance (Piper and Cash)

Last Call: A Marriage of Convenience Romance (Esther and Koa)

Binge the following series in eBook, paperback, or audio!

Brady Family Series

Foundation: A Grouchy Geek Romance (Zack and Nicole)

Suspension: An Opposites Attract Romance (Liam and Maddie)

Inspection: A Silver Fox Romance (Kellen and Elizabeth)

Vibration: An Accidental Roommates Romance (Cal and Logan)

Current: A Secret Baby Romance (Orla and Walt)

Restoration: A Silver Fox Redemption Romance (Mick and Celeste)

Oak Creek Series

The Nerd and the Neighbor (Hunter and Abigail)

The Botanist and the Billionaire (Diana and Asa)

The Midwife and the Money (Archer and Opal)

The Planner and the Player (Fletcher and Thistle)

Stag Brothers Series

Sweet Distraction (Tim and Alice)

Filled Potential (Ty and Juniper)

Fragile Illusion (Thatcher and Emma)

A Stag Family Christmas

Beautiful Game (Hawk and Lucy)

Stag Generations Series

Forging Passion (Wes and Cara prequel)

Forging Glory (Wes and Cara)

Forging Legacy (Wyatt and Fern)

Forging Chaos (coming soon)

Stone Creek University

Deep in the Pocket: A Football Romance

Hard Edge: A Hockey Romance

Possession: A Football Romance

Made in United States
North Haven, CT
24 May 2024